DIASPORA DREAMS

ANDREW CHATORA

Kharis Publishing, an imprint of Kharis Media LLC

Copyright © 2021 ANDREW CHATORA

ISBN-13: 978-1-63746-029-0
ISBN-10: 1-63746-029-5

Library of Congress Control Number:2021933837

All rights reserved. This book or parts thereof may not be reproduced in any form, stored in a retrieval system, or transmitted in any form by any means - electronic, mechanical, photocopy, recording, or otherwise - without prior written permission of the publisher, except as provided by United States of America copyright law.

Unless otherwise noted, Scripture taken from the New American Standard Bible®, copyright © 1960,1962,1963,1968,1971,1972,1973,1975,1977,1995 by The Lockman Foundation. Used by permission.

All KHARIS PUBLISHING products are available at special quantity discounts for bulk purchase for sales promotions, premiums, fundraising, and educational needs. For details, contact:

Kharis Media LLC
Tel: 1-479-599-8657
support@kharispublishing.com
www.kharispublishing.com

To my siblings,
Deliah, Naume, Fiona, Arthur, Wadzanai
With love

CONTENTS

Title Page
Copyright
Dedication
Foreword
Chapter 1 — 1
Chapter 2 — 9
Chapter 3 — 17
Chapter 4 — 23
Chapter 5 — 37
Chapter 6 — 45
Chapter 7 — 52
Chapter 8 — 56
Chapter 9 — 67
Chapter 10 — 73
Chapter 11 — 85
Chapter 12 — 90
Chapter 13 — 95
Chapter 14 — 105
Chapter 15 — 118
Chapter 16 — 124
Chapter 17 — 132

Chapter 18	135
Chapter 19	142
Chapter 20	159
Acknowledgments	167
About The Author	169
Praise For Author	171
ABOUT KHARIS PUBLISHING	173
New Book Coming Soon…	175
I	177
II	183
III	187
IV	189
V	193

FOREWORD

Anatomy of Hope

Back in April 2020, in the throes of lockdown in my serene Milton Keynes flat, I embarked on the proverbial journey of a thousand miles of landmark trail, writing my debut novella which increasingly has strayed into novel territory. And even now the title has undergone so much change, from ***Dreams from Zimbabwe ~ Memoirs of an English Teacher***, to ***Broken Amniotic Fluid***, to now simply, ***Diaspora Dreams***, though part of me keeps flirting with ***Anatomy of Dreams*** as an alternative title.

Dream big or go home, I thought. I'm a firm believer that, if you create something you believe is good, great... throw it out there to be judged, critiqued, praised. If we don't, how can we grow as writers?

Looking back at how 2020 developed into one of the most bizarre years I can remember in my lifetime, I guess it wasn't such an outlandish shot to take, especially now, as I stand on the threshold of my manuscript being published. The immigrant experience is a story worth telling, one for which I am willing to stick my neck out above the parapet and share with fellow global citizens. I will always maintain our stories should never be forgotten. The heroism and the desperate struggles many of our people have had to endure in their adopted homes the world over should forever be kept green in the memory of posterity. This is the remit I seek to achieve in *Diaspora Dreams*. I wish to extend my utmost gratitude to various people who have made this project so close to my heart come to fruition.

CHAPTER 1

The Dream

I have capacity. How else have I managed to keep my thoughts consistently in my secret diary, and yet the powers that be, continue to misrepresent my persona? I silently mused to myself.

I arrived in England on a freezing March morning circa 2002, aboard a South African Airways flight. I felt nervous as I made the long walk to the immigration exit point. "Good luck," a young white couple, who had sat next to me on the eleven-hour flight from Johannesburg, South Africa, politely whispered in my ear, as I prepared to disembark from the plane. Perhaps they had sussed me out: wet behind the ears, a newbie, out to try my luck in entering England for my fair share of what is termed, "the American dream," across the transatlantic in the United States.

I hadn't had the guts to ask the couple their names. All I remember was them telling me they lived in Greater London, and they were coming from their honeymoon. Part of my trepidation at approaching the immigration checkpoint at Heathrow Airport was mainly because a lot hinged on my gaining entry to the United Kingdom. I was a fugitive from Zimbabwe, a country I loved dearly, but had sadly given up on. My departure, personally, historically, and ideologically, followed the litany of political mismanagement by those at the helm of power, since its independence, attained from colonial Britain in 1980.

Crushed hopes and dreams! That just about summed up the

post-colonial Zimbabwe experience for me. Talk of independence irritated me now, as it had become synonymous with organized crime and an attendant band of self-serving, bloodthirsty occultists with an unbridled sense of entitlement to pillaging Zimbabwe's resources ad infinitum; there had been no reprisals, let alone accountability, to the electorate. Every now and then, in five-year intervals, a sprinkling of sham elections would be held, as if to appease the international community with a semblance of multi-party democracy. These election charades were usually accompanied by an orgy of well-orchestrated, systematic violence and bloodbaths employed to coerce, instill fear in, and intimidate citizens to be cowed into voting for a perpetuation of the same old - same old, the clueless dinosaur establishment. Why would I want to go back?

There was also a plethora of other reasons I simply could not fathom returning to Zimbabwe. I had unceremoniously called time on my teaching career. My wife, Kay, was heavily pregnant with our soon-to-be first child due in May. Kay had left Zimbabwe four months earlier than me; she also had sought to escape the economic woes and hardships which had become analogous with our country of birth. We shared a dream: to better our lives, which we accepted wouldn't be possible in our motherland, given our calling, both as high school teachers, and our employers' well-documented *laissez fare* attitude towards our vocation.

As I shuffled in the Heathrow immigration queue, clutching my green Zimbabwean passport, *green bomber*, as we called it, with my ugly, sprawly handwriting protruding from the landing card, I strove to give off confident vibes. The constant tutelage was all too fresh in my mind from friends, family and colleagues, all *ghetto wiseacres*. Each one was a mountebank with anecdotal stories of how to get it right the first time with immigration officers at London Heathrow Airport, lest one be deported, there and then, on the next flight back home. My arrival was a morning flight; we landed at 6:15 am, which in Zimbabwe was quarter past eight in the morning. I knew they were all praying for a safe passage for me, back at N 133 A Dangamvura, Mutare. That is, my family was praying for me so their first-born son would make it in the land of the Queen. The assumption was once, Kundai made it; *nesuwo tapinda,* as we said in our mother tongue, meaning we would become both affluent and the envy of all and sundry within the vicinity.

Never underestimate how England is perceived in developing countries the world over. Zimbabwe is certainly no exception in this regard. So, here I was with the weight of the Mafirakureva clan's expectations weighing heavily on my lean shoulders. With their prayers, what could go wrong? "Next," the airport usher's friendly voice jolted me out of the reverie. I was jellyfish inside as I walked to Immigration Counter 6. Glancing up, I saw the immigration officer was a middle-aged, bespectacled white woman with a face like Michael Jackson. She spoke sharply at me in an intimidating way, "Good morning and welcome to England." She stretched out her hand, beckoning, "Passport please." Peering intently at me, she stated, rather than asked, "Can you please state the purpose of your visit."

"Ahm, ah, I'm visiting my wife," I mumbled furtively, then muttered, "My wife is a teacher here, and I'm here to support her, as she is pregnant." My confidence now sky-high, I had quickly regained my composure.

I reflected on prior advice from those self-proclaimed township immigration wiseacres in my Dangamvura hood, who had persistently admonished me that under no circumstance should I dare approach a black immigration officer. This would be one sure way to be sent back home. "Black immigration officers are the worst, Kuu, steer clear of them at Heathrow. They're not on your side; you're better off dealing with a white immigration officer," they had admonished, and here I was, talking to this English woman with her cutglass accent.

She went on with her barrage of questions in a fast and loose downpour of clipped verbal bits. She asked, "How can I trust that you'll return to Zimbabwe after visiting your wife?"

I fished from my hand luggage a letter from my employer which stated I was on official leave. I couldn't read the woman's body language, as she didn't give anything away. Nevertheless, she kept scribbling furiously and glancing on the computer screen in front of her. Calmly, the bombshell came: "I am not satisfied with your reasons for visiting England, and will have to detain you, under section blah, blah, dash blah, as I need to ask you further questions. Can you step aside, please, and sit by that bench," she said, motioning to a bench behind me, where two young Chinese youngsters were huddled, most likely, I thought, in a similar scenario. My heart skipped and somersaulted. I couldn't quite understand what had just happened to this immigration woman to effect so sudden a change in her demeanour.

Had she found something untoward about my intentions on her computer screen? How could this be? Could it be that she was one of those psychics? These and a whole host of other questions flooded my psyche. However, I didn't have to wait long. I was soon escorted and ushered into another adjoining room by overly officious security guards with bloodshot eyes who glared menacingly at me. There was no pretense they liked me here. In the room to which they shepherded me sat a man and a woman; she was sobbing uncontrollably as the man remonstrated his intentions as a bona fide UK visitor. He flung and wrung his hands in the air as if to convince immigration officialdom of his credibility. One never easily flustered, I managed to regain my self-assurance again, and was doing my best to sound level-headed. At that point, however, the female immigration officer charged into the room dramatically and beckoned to speak with me.

As I stepped aside, she brandished my passport at me and blurted, "I have given you a six- month visitor's visa. I have spoken with your wife. I am satisfied you are a genuine visitor. I do, however, have to emphasize to you that you are not allowed to work or claim public funds for the duration of your visit, and you must return to Zimbabwe at the end of your visitor's visa term." She may as well have been babbling by then. I was caught in a vortex of ecstasy, realizing I had made it into England to be with my Kay and our unborn child!

Always a grandmaster at hiding my body language, I politely thanked the Michael Jackson lookalike woman and asked her for directions out of the immigration alcove. She pointed me in the opposite direction to where we were standing, admonishing, "Your wife is waiting for you by the Arrivals area."

And so, I quickly collected my luggage from the revolving escalator and made a brisk dash for the Arrivals section. Good old Kay was easily identifiable as much by her bulging tummy of seven months pregnancy, as by her beautiful, dimpled smile as she peered at me from behind her glasses. *So, I did love Kay at one point then, with genuine, unadulterated love,* I mused to myself. *Hear, hear, I did love Kay, do you hear me?* I started laughing uncontrollably and wondered why others were staring at me askance.

We had a long, emotional hug and embrace. Kay was all choked up, crying at seeing me again, as she enquired, "How was your flight?"

"Generally okay. Glad, I made it," I chuckled. I gave her the immigration drama lowdown once we were firmly ensconced on the London underground train heading towards North London, Edmonton. Kay informed me we were going to be living with her sister Nyarai, a nurse in North London. Apparently, Nyarai had been exceedingly kind and volunteered to shelter us at her house until we got ourselves sorted.

I must admit I was dazzled and mesmerized by many things on this, my maiden journey in England. First time on the tube, everything seemed so strange and surreal. I was visibly awestruck with so much novelty, and Kay took it upon herself to be my initiator and leading light, explaining and pointing out all the familiar landmarks, like the Seven Sisters and Camden Market, among others. Upon our arrival at Edmonton, Nyarai gave us a lukewarm response, but I didn't make much of it at the time, except it was somehow at variance with the glowing accounts Kay had given me of *sisi* Nyari and her kind-hearted nature. I had no time for trivia at that point. I hadn't seen my wife in nearly five months. All I wanted was for some quality time together, alone in the privacy of our bedroom. Who cares about grumpy old sister Nyari?

That night with Kay, we did it like freshman students. It was slow, patient, hot and passionate. Considering she was seven months pregnant; I couldn't comprehend where Kay got the physical strength and stamina for our nooky that night. Tired and spent, we drifted off to sleep. What could go wrong when I had now been reunited with my wife?

Loud voices woke me up at about six in the morning on my second day in England. I turned over in the double bed, trying to feel for Kay. She was nowhere to be found. It was then I craned my ears again, tiptoed to the slightly open door, and heard the angry exchange between Kay and her supposedly good-natured sister, Nyari.

"Things are tough here in England. You are pregnant and not working. I can't look after you and your husband. You have to quickly make plans and leave today. My daughter Tawana needs her bedroom where you slept with Kundai," bellowed sisi Nyari in a high-pitched tone. There was not even an attempt by Nyari to speak quietly. I reckoned she wanted to drive home her message, loud and clear. Now was not the time for equivocation.

As I stood, frozen in my tracks, trying to process this earth-shattering news to my eardrums, I heard Kay giving it back in equal measure, "But, sisi Nyari, that's so underhanded and unfair. You did promise me Kundai and I would stay here until I get another job. How can you do this to me?"

I was suddenly caught up in a tsunami of emotions. Talk about information overload! So many things were happening all at once for my formerly euphoric brain to process. What did sisi Nyari mean, Kay didn't have a job? Surely, she was mistaken; Kay had got a long-term teaching job whilst she was still in Zimbabwe; her work permit had been couriered to her by DHL. And if for one minute that were true, Kay would have been upfront with me and told me. Kay had always been open with me. We operated an open-door policy in our marriage, or so I thought. Was my world falling apart, already? What was happening, so soon, when I was still in my honeymoon phase of arrival in England? All these unanswered questions raced through my bewildered mind. As I could neither contain my anxiety nor stand the bickering voices downstairs, I decided to confront the lion's den. I made some polite coughs as I went downstairs to the two women to give them prior warning of my imminent entry. But *sisi* Nyari was in a foul temper that morning. In retrospect, we may have pissed her off with our noisy lovemaking the previous night and she just about snapped and lost it with us.

To cut a long story short, by mid-morning both Kay and I had been unceremoniously kicked out of the Edmonton flat by a supposedly "kind" woman with a "heart of gold." And so, it happened, Kay and I took our few belongings and headed out of the place where we were unwanted. I didn't even have the chance to phone my folks back home in Mutare to let them know I had made it, courtesy of their prayers and warm wishes.

Kay was smart. She could see I was seething with anger. As it appeared, she owed me a credible explanation on her "not working" status that sisi Nyari had blurted out, not to mention our surreal eviction from the flat. "Time to come clean, my love," I chided her.

She explained she'd lost her job at the West London School soon after arriving in England. She said, "I couldn't tell you, because I didn't want to worry you, but the silver lining is, my teaching agency has arranged a job for me in Aylesbury Town in Buckinghamshire. I'm supposed to start on Tuesday and hadn't had time to tell sisi Nyari. But anyway, you saw it yourself, how she acted this morning, quite a complete somersault from her earlier promise to look out after us."

I commiserated with Kay, squeezed her hand and assured her, "All will be well, sweetheart. We will get over this setback, trust me." Inwardly, though, I started to worry about money. Now that I knew Kay hadn't been working for some time, and wasn't drawing any salary, the cold reality became palpable to me: We would urgently need money for rent and food. Now that Kay had shared with me the prospect of a new job the following Tuesday, we still needed money for the train fare to Aylesbury and rent money or hotel money. Goodness knows, we didn't know anyone else who could help us. We'd just been made homeless against our will. "Between me and poverty, I have the £200 I came with from Zimbabwe as spending money, so, we can use this as a starting point," I blurted out to Kay. She rummaged in her handbag and managed to fish out three, creased twenty-pound notes and a fiver, so that bumped up our money to two hundred and sixty-five quid.

It was at that point that Kay remembered she had a Barclaycard credit card, and so on our way to the London underground, we made a detour into Barclays Bank. Kay was able to replenish our family coffers. We made our nascent trip to Aylesbury, which was to be our home for several years to come.

CHAPTER 2

Aylesbury

Kay and I arrived in Aylesbury on a Friday after 4pm. It was a brave journey for both of us, as we didn't know anyone in the town. Of course, the pull factor was Kay's imminent teaching job, due to start the coming Tuesday at the local Quarrendon Upper School. Years later, Kay and I always looked back and chuckled at our bravado, as "We didn't even know where we were going to sleep that night."

As it happened, upon disembarking from the train, I inquired the whereabouts of a tourist shop from a kind stranger who gave us comprehensive, precise directions. It was ten to 5pm when we both walked into Aylesbury Tourist Information Center, but the woman in there nearly shooshed us out, as she was already closing for the day. "Please, we are strangers in Aylesbury," we pleaded, "Can you recommend any bed and breakfast, reasonable prices?" Although she had been somewhat unhappy at seeing us, the woman rose to the occasion, phoning several B & Bs which were sadly full. "Goodness gracious me," I interposed impatiently, "Why is the town so popular?" On the stroke of 5pm, we made our first breakthrough; the woman managed to lodge us at Bierton Bed and Breakfast, which was close to town and was charging £35 for bed and breakfast. A taxi ferried us to our new home along Bierton Road.

Unbeknownst to us, we were later to live down the road on a similar street to Bierton Road. Janice, our landlady, was quite a plump and cheerful woman. It took Kay to tell me she was pregnant; it was her first pregnancy, a fact the openly excited Janice shared with us the next morning as she served our measly breakfast of cereal, tea, and an array of assorted biscuits. The breakfast wasn't much to write home about, as Kay and I mostly had steaming hot mugs of coffee served with toast on marmalade and I managed to prepare scrambled eggs in the microwave as an extra for Kay, as I really wanted to wait on her, spoil her a lot on account of her pregnancy. I reckoned my pretty young wife needed humoring around, as we'd been apart from each other for several months. I wouldn't hear of it when she protested at the attention, I was lavishing her with, "You really don't need to wait on me that much Kundai, I can still do things for myself you know?"

"Of course, I know you can Muffin, but now is my time to look out after you love, and pamper you, for missing out when I was in Zim, and you were here by yourself," I had remarked as I gave her a smacker on the forehead. "Here, have some more toast, mind you, we may go out for the day shortly, who knows?" I remarked as I shoved more toast in Kay's plate.

"Okay, I give up, handsome, I see you've got a plan to fatten me up, the pregnancy isn't simply big enough for you, is it?" she'd grudgingly relented, as she shovelled more toast and scrambled eggs into her mouth, much to my delight.

"Good, now we're in business," I chuckled back at her, glad to see her take more food portions. Soon after breakfast, Kay decided she wanted to familiarize herself with her new school, as they were expecting her in two days' time. Janice was good with the directions she gave us, adding, "You don't need a taxi. It's 10 minutes or so from here, though Kay should take it easy." Janice nodded knowingly, staring at Kay's protruding belly.

The greater part of that morning we walked leisurely to Quarrendon School, which would be Kay's new employers and possibly save us from imminent bankruptcy. The school was set on imposing grounds with sprawling, multi-story buildings; it was a far cry from our single, dormitory type or block classrooms in Zimbabwe. I don't know whether it was because I was still new myself in the country, but everything I came across and experienced looked new. Talk of novelty, there was the omnipresent fleet of vehicles. "Oh my god," remarked Kay, excitedly tugging at my cardigan, "Do you see that Kuu?" She pointed to the avalanche of vehicles whizzing past us as we trudged along the pavement. I must admit, the sheer volume of traffic was massive, and the vehicles mostly looked fancy. Seeing those avalanches of cars with Kay was quite something. Back then, I had never contemplated that one day in England, I too would be steering my way confidently in the M25 motorway traffic, switching and maneuvering between lanes easily.

By the time we returned "home," it was already late afternoon. Poor Kay was visibly washed out with the walking and I felt for her. "You need to rest, *love*, get yourself a well-deserved siesta," I remarked. "I will organize some takeaways for dinner." Janice had reiterated to us that she wouldn't serve any meals other than breakfast. I know we hadn't been that long at Janice's B & B, but the monotony of only having a mostly cold breakfast without the likelihood of a hot evening meal was already beginning to grate on us. In addition, we also missed *sadza,* our staple diet from mealie meal, which now was a mere pipe dream. That evening, I ordered some hot chicken and wings with *jolofu* rice which, I must say, we thoroughly enjoyed.

The weekend quickly passed, and before we knew it, Tuesday was upon us. I accompanied Kay to her new workplace. The sting of the new workplace soon became evident in the evening, when Kay said she'd liked the school and her new colleagues. The only setback was that she was due to deliver in May. They couldn't offer her a full-time contract but could only employ her as a supply teacher, and she would be paid weekly. I tried to reassure her, "It's better than not getting anything at all. In time, they may give you a permanent contract after your delivery. Who knows?"

"You never know," Kay retorted sarcastically.

We started to think of looking for accommodations elsewhere, as £35 quid a day was not something we could afford in the long run, despite the assurance of Kay getting a weekly salary. So, we made plans. During the day, when Kay was at work, I would phone around and inquire for houses through both estate agents and individual landlords. Once an intellectual, always an intellectual; I don't know how I did it but in no time, I had made my inquiries and I knew where the local Aylesbury library was. I used to frequent it during the day when Kay was at work and I'd use their free online service to browse the internet and check out accommodation, sending emails to prospective landlords.

With her first paycheck, Kay bought me a mobile phone, an Ericson 628, which was quite a beauty then. I still have fond memories of it, my first ever mobile phone. I made several phone calls before we managed to get accommodation. Perhaps the deal breaker was my naivete, which meant I blurted out my personal business to every Tom, Dick and Josh prospective landlord about Kay being heavily pregnant. At that point, no one became interested. Of course, there was that case of false hope when Janice booked us to see a high street estate agent in Aylesbury town centre. Kay and I excitedly called in at Harlet Estate Agents and met up with sales negotiator Gillian, who was a bundle of energy and all smiles. Unbeknownst to us, there was a rigorous, pre-vetting exercise which we failed, mainly because of Kay's employment status as a supply teacher on a supply contract, which the agency deemed not secure. So ended our fanciful dreams of moving into a posh Aylesbury flat. It was back to the house-hunting drawing board again.

We eventually managed to make a breakthrough one Thursday evening when I spoke with Glen Garrick. Kay and I both went to see the room. It was a small, one-bedroom in a shared house with four other tenants: Albert the Ghanaian fella, Pretty and Lorraine, two Zimbabwean girls who shared a room, and Steve

Vickers, the eccentric Bohemian alcoholic from Cornwall.

"So, do you like it?" asked Glen.

"Liked it," we said, exchanging knowing glances. "Of course, we like it." We didn't have a choice. That was how we moved into 14 St. Catherine's Court, Prebendal Estate, where our daughter Alexis was born.

Kay settled into the mundane routine of her teaching job at Quarrendon. The months quickly flew by. Kay's delivery became imminent with each passing day. The health visitor had done a proper job, dutifully attending to Kay during her antenatal period. "You have the option to deliver at home, but it doesn't look like a good idea to me," Sarah the health visitor had tactfully intimated to Kay. Later, we both chuckled at her subtle tact.

"It sure didn't come as a surprise to me, Kuu," Kay remarked. "Sarah clearly saw our squalid living conditions here at St. Catherine's Court, and no way would she have sanctioned that I give birth here." So, the waiting game carried on for the expected delivery date.

We didn't stay long at St. Catherine's Court following the birth of Alexis. I bet Kay and I both knew, in our heart of hearts, the St. Catherine's Court set-up wasn't ideal for a family, it being a miserably small room. In addition, grumpy old git Glen made it clear he wasn't happy when he realized Kay was pregnant, so I had quietened him down with the, "We will leave soon" promise. We eventually did leave and moved into our own two-bedroom flat in Bierton Road. The wheel was coming full circle, pretty full on, as we were now a stone's throw away from our former B & B landlord Janice's place.

After Kay's delivery, our money woes as a family came to the fore again. Kay had to stop her supply teaching, and with that came the attendant drying of our family coffers. Suddenly, that dread and money worry was back on me as the proverbial head of the house. I felt I had a paternal duty to provide for my missus Kay and our new-born daughter, Alexis. Throw into the mix a six-month visitor's visa, which effectively outlawed me from working, and we were both in a complete fix with no apparent outlet. Albert, good old Albert, my Ghanaian housemate, saved the day for us.

Through Albert's kind intervention, I got a job working alongside him and his mate, Mike, as a co-valet at Assured Valeting, a makeshift tent behind the popular Bicester Road, Aylesbury Audi garage. There, we washed cars for the posh and affluent and gave them a thorough cleaning, both inside and out. It was a hard, back-breaking, physically excruciating job, at which I recoil, thinking of it now. The toil made such an impact on my physical stamina and self-esteem. It made a permanent dent in my intellectualism. I bore the brunt of my two work mates' self-styled black on white racism and parochialism, even though, ironically, Mike touted himself as Assured Valeting's proprietor. He tended to prey on old white women, mostly single mothers, so he could live off them and particularly live rent free. Such a calculating, predatory monster. So, at night he was shagging the very people he purported to despise, but by day he would be spouting anti-white venom to me. Maybe he thought it made him look cool to me, as I was new in the country.

Looking back, I think he may have been bitter and nursing a relationship breakdown hangover. His previous white girlfriend had kicked him out of the house, even though they had a daughter called Zara together. That he was still in love with her was as clear as daylight. Once, she came to have her car valeted and Mike took ages on it. He could almost lick that car, the way he went on about it.

Things were also not helped by how both Mike and Albert used to bully me to make themselves feel better about themselves. We got paid £3 for each car we valeted, but there was an exception for bigger cars, which fetched £6; both Mike and Albert made sure that these bigger vehicles were their preserve alone. Once I tried dissenting, but Mike promptly put me in my place in a heavy-handed fashion, with threats of instigating my deportation. "Aaah, aaah mister, don't forget you're working here on account of my goodwill. I could have you deported you know. You're not meant to be working at all, so don't forget yourself son," he said, gleefully pacing throughout the sweltering hot tent, arms behind his back, his malevolent lips curling into a sadistic smile. That was enough to quieten me.

Then, there was that fateful Monday morning I was late at work because of childcare issues; Kay needed some last-minute help, and lo and behold, all hell broke loose that morning when I arrived at Assured Valeting Garage at twelve minutes past 9am. I was given a humiliating, condescending dressing down by Mike, which was nigh draconian and disproportionate to one being late for work by a few minutes, yet one has a legitimate reason for this. "Now Kundai, let me tell you this, and I will tell you this for nuffing; some home truths once and for all," began Mike in his condescending tone as he walked up and down the huge, white marquee which housed the cars we cleaned with a caricatured air of exaggerated self-confidence. "You're 12 minutes late, Kundai. You know very well that the job starts at 9am on the dot, yet you decided to waltz in your fat ass lackadaisically and well after 9am. How is this?" He spoke as he glared at me menacingly.

"I...I... I had child care emergency," I stuttered, as my fear and loathing for Mike overwhelmed me, and yet he wasn't yet done with me that morning, as he tore into me like a feral beast.

"Childcare problems huh! How is that my problem? You look at me and Albert, day in, day out, we're here at 9am on the dot, without fail. You think we don't have our issues and shit to deal with? Now listen and listen to me proper, Kundai; consider this your final warning. If this ever happens again, you are out, do you hear me lazy bones? I said, you're out!" He bawled at me at the top of his voice as he appeared to have lost it completely. I mumbled my apologies under my breath and quietly retreated to valeting my first car of the day. That entire nine hour shift we worked in complete and utter silence and I was glad to retire home where I shared my travails with my Muffin, Kay in the comfort of her bosom.

The flipside hypocrisy to Mike's unreasonable diatribe against me was spectacularly played out in stark contrast a few months later when the 2002 world cup football competition commenced. Because football matches were flighted on television during the day, at a time we were at work, Mike and his acquiescing side kick Albert devised a clever plan whereby, each of the day for the duration of the world cup, they would dodge work and drive off to go and watch live football matches and yet left me in the line of duty, in charge of valeting customer cars by myself. I know when I'm beaten and chose not to rock the boat. Equally, I knew very well the wisdom of the proverbial statement, *let sleeping dogs lie, or one has to pick their battles very carefully, lest my pettiness became my nemesis, the chink in one's armor,* thus I tactfully held my tongue, and for good reason.

Back home in Zimbabwe, early on in my life, my late father, m'koma John, had inculcated in me the work ethic, so I lumped on with it. I was pragmatic enough and inwardly acknowledged that the valeting job served a purpose. For want of a cliché, it kept the family afloat, between Kay's maternity break till she resumed work in September, which turned out brilliantly. I eventually landed a teaching job at Brackley Community College for a September start, much to the chagrin of Albert and Mike.

CHAPTER 3

Shipwreck

Settling down in Aylesbury town, Buckinghamshire, brought its own challenges, not least of which were marital difficulties with Kay. Looking back, I am not sure at what point cracks started to emerge in our relationship. All I know is that marriage to Kay increasingly became a stifling prison for me which I wanted to escape. I was tired of the endless bickering, silly mind games, and needless arguments. At times, I felt she wielded too much power in the marriage. The relationship was lopsided against me. Perhaps I resented Kay for earning more money than I; this was quite a huge reversal of fortunes from when we worked in Zimbabwe. Inwardly, I felt Kay was challenging my masculinity now that her salary was way ahead of mine. She tried to exercise her newfound dominance in the marriage by sometimes making unilateral decisions without even asking my input on matters which also impacted on me. I felt muted in the marriage, as if my voice did not matter. Once I picked a quarrel with her and blamed her for making me leave my beloved Zimbabwe, driving me away from my family and making me live in this perpetually cold country.

"You should just have left me in my home comfort zone," I said.

"Really, Kundai, are you sure of that?" Kay countered.

"Why wouldn't I be?" I rudely retorted.

But how did we come to be this, a couple who had sat down, planned, and carved out our dreams in rural Tsonzo High School in Mutasa district where we both taught? Disillusioned with Mugabe's disastrous and ruinous economic policies, we had been brutally honest to each other: Zimbabwe had no future for us or any children we were likely to have. Against this backdrop, we made emigrating to England our topmost priority. Kay would go first, then I would follow later. Kay going first was more of a leap of faith, taking a plunge in the darkness, as she was already a few months pregnant when she got her teaching post in England.

Over the years, it has increasingly been difficult to pinpoint one single reason why our union soured so quickly. There are moments when I think I get it, but even now, I am not so sure anymore. *By and by, Kundai thinks he gets it, but he doesn't.* I know the overbearing family demands and expectations from Zimbabwe also took their toll on the marriage, but to what extent did both of us play a part in the dissolution? Hand on heart, can we say we really tried hard enough to preserve the nuptials? Did we try, as responsible adults, to sit down, brush aside our inflated egos, look each other in the eye, and talk and thrash out our differences, if not for us but for the sake of Alexis and Brooklyn?

My mother bless her heart, for she is my conscience and moral compass, many a time questioned me on the wisdom of buying the Lay Road matrimonial home, given my incessant squabbles with Kay.

"Son, I pre-warned you countless times not to enter into a mortgage with this woman, given your well-documented squabbling," Mother would often remark to me at the height of my marital woes with Kay. I didn't know how to answer her entreaties, for inwardly I knew she'd been correct in sussing out her daughter-in-law's shortcomings. Mothers have an intuitive way of reading people's character traits correctly, more so if it's a woman their son has chosen to be a spouse, and I'm afraid Mother was spot on in her estimation of wily Kay. Equally so, she'd been on point in the scepticism she'd exhibited and privately shared with me, when I'd brought Kay home for introductions as the girl I wanted to marry and commit to. Yet against Mother's wisdom, which was well-founded as the events of later years were to vindicate her disquietude; bizarrely, perhaps it was more of irrational defiance. I had gone ahead and married Kay anyway, even though some of the red flags had been clearly palpable to me.

But why did I act irrationally? I don't know. I justify some of my irrational decisions with Kay, which made me hang on for 13 good years of my life with her, even though the writing was clearly on the wall that it was finished. But I still soldiered on. I give that to love. Twisted love, some would say. How can you live with your "tormentor" under the same roof? I mean, how does it even work, unless you are a masochist? The more erudite amongst my friends gave it a fancy name: Stockholm Syndrome love. Well, perhaps it was my love for the children and the need to provide stability for them by ensuring they had both parents together. Still, even that proved counterproductive in the end, as the squabbling escalated to unprecedented levels.

The marriage quickly degenerated into a dysfunctional farce in which Kay and I resented each other. I don't think it was that we didn't try hard enough. We did a stint with Relate Counselling. Unfortunately, that backfired on me, once Kay started yelling back at me in an argument, "You are doing exactly what the Relate woman said you shouldn't do, telling me what to do. You are not my father."

So that was it; I refused to go back to Relate Counselling if "everything was my fault" and I was to be used as a prop in any future domestic dispute we had. In line with our African culture and values, we sought assistance from the family elders; god knows how many *matare* or family-sanctioned mediation courts to which Kay and I subjected ourselves, but to no avail. In later years, I was to remark at the wisdom in words uttered by a good friend Roland: "*Some things can't be fixed Kundai.*" And

I'm afraid, with hindsight, that may have been the case with Kay and me; things just couldn't work in the end, given the best will and intentions.

"You never take us out; we never go on holiday. Honestly, Kundai, this marriage has never taken precedence with you. It's always been those people first."

"Which people?" I impatiently interrupted her.

"What do you care to know, so you can go and demonize me again to your mother!"

She knew I hated it each time she referred to Mbuya Mafirakureva as "your mother." Of course, she was my mother, but there was something condescending and demeaning in the way Kay uttered the phrase, *"your mother."* Once, I had jumped down her throat when she started banging on about my widowed mum being a leech on our family resources. Ever since that day, she kept saying, *"your mother,"* in that odious tone of hers, most likely to annoy me, as she was well-aware of how it riled me. And in any slightest argument we had, she would use it to threaten calling the police on me with, "Don't you dare raise your voice at me Kundai, or else!"

"Or else what?"

"You know me, I won't hesitate to call the police on you, and you know what the police are like in this country. You are a black man. I am most likely to be believed over you."

Inwardly, I knew she was spot on, especially having seen how other black males with vengeful spouses had been at the mercy and receiving end of malicious, false allegations of domestic abuse from their vindictive partners. I hated her more for the way she said, "You know me," speaking as if it were a badge of honor to falsely snitch on one's husband.

"Others are buying second, third, holiday homes in Spain, and all you ever think is blooming Zimbabwe."

"Well, I'm not others, am I?" I snapped angrily at Kay. "I'm my own man. Why didn't you get married to those social climbers then?" I began to get increasingly annoyed with her whining and needless nit-picking of my Zim family. *Who does she think she is? How dare she take on my family like that?* I certainly took great exception to her insouciance.

"This is not normal," Kay yelled at me, "And you appear to be the only one in town oblivious to this brazen, weird set-up, where you put others who live thousands of miles away from you first, and yet…and yet, you put their interests ahead of your own immediate family. Even my friend, Mai Tawanda, admits you're a twisted oddball."

Kay barrelled on, "Mai Tawanda goes on expensive holidays within and beyond Europe; she's all designer from designer handbags, wears designer clothes, designer lingerie, yet I have to rely on second-hand charity shop clothes and apparel. I have come to the conclusion that you actually despise me, Kundai. You never show me any love or affection; the only time you show me love is when you want to get inside me."

And with those sentiments, she would shed her crocodile tears. That was classic, vintage Kay, trying to emotionally blackmail me so I could play ball and be her acquiescing puppet. But I had long wizened up to her silly antics and I wasn't going to let her tie me round her slimy, manipulative, little fingers anymore. So oftentimes, I let these puerile mind games just pass.

My mother, Mbuya Mafirakureva, when she visited us in 2008, also tried brokering conciliation and mediation talks on our behalf through her church. But even *gogo's* magic wand failed to work on us. Perhaps our union was doomed; we were both headstrong characters, Kay and I, though I hate saying this, as it reeks of nihilism and pessimism. There was indeed a clash of family values between my side and Kay's side of the family, my family being accused as money mongers, constantly feasting and bleeding on the family pot. Although, I could say the same of Kay's family, by slinging the mud back at her avaricious lot, particularly her mother, Fugude. It was a classic case of the pot calling the kettle black. But in all honesty, Kay also had her personal demons to deal with, not least of which was her split personality, bipolar disorder, which was to later ruin her relationship with our daughter, Alexis. You couldn't make that stuff up with Kay. One minute she could be charming, sweet, and pleasant, then, within a split second, she could become vicious and nasty, a feral beast. I know what I am talking about. I bore the brunt of this for over a decade of my life.

As things escalated and became increasingly unbearable during the tenure of Mbuya Mafirakureva, my mother's visit to us, she once exploded to her irate daughter in law, "Do you think Kundai just fell from the heavens, just like that?"

"Kundai has relations in Zimbabwe. Now, I don't want to interfere in your marriage, but it's about time you know this *muroora*, the bonds of family are far stronger and more sacrosanct than to be severed by *mutorwa*, an outsider, *mudzimai*. I am also married to the Mafirakureva family; for over three score years, I know this dictum quite well. Let he who has ears listen and take heed." And that pretty much summed up mother's wise counsel to a bemused Kay who, for once, remained tongue-tied.

CHAPTER 4

Pressure from Home: Kundai of Old

In our African culture, particularly among the Shona people, from whom I originated, it is the expectation and the norm that elder children look after their aged parents and other siblings, both materially and financially. This is all the more so when the father of the house may have passed on, which was the scenario for me. This was quite a different culture from the English way of life, as I've noticed over the two decades I've lived here. Seeking to understand other variables which may have contributed to the breakdown of my marriage with Kay, pressures from Zimbabwe certainly did play a central role, both from my side and hers. Earlier, I alluded to the Mafirakureva clan's expectations weighing heavily on my shoulders when I arrived in England on my maiden flight. Such may also have been the case with Kay's rapacious family, particularly her conniving, scheming mother, Fugude.

For some of us who emigrated to the United Kingdom in the early 2000s, the impact of Zimbabweans who flocked to the UK in the early to mid-90s, then returned home to visit, was far from positive or beneficial. It didn't help our case that those earlier Zimbabweans who flocked to the UK as the political and economic crisis in Zimbabwe deepened, flashed a flamboyant, glamorous lifestyle each time they came home from England. They often drank large, and spent big, buying retail property in upmarket suburbs. Consequently, the mainstream thinking in Zimbabwe became: "If you want to make it big, then the diaspora (as they called it, particularly in the UK) is the way to go." Because of the prevalence of the Zimbabwean community in England, the UK became nicknamed, "Harare North," as if it were an extension of Harare, Zimbabwe's capital city.

For me, the warning signs that avarice and greed would ruin my marriage presented themselves early on. The day before I departed for England, Kay's family, by no means privileged themselves but not in any want, phoned me and demanded I leave them the television and wardrobe from our matrimonial household goods. Their reasoning was: Kay had bought both items, so her family should have them. Never mind that I was already married to their daughter when she bought the TV and wardrobe, and I rightfully considered them marital property. Add to that my fiery temperament; I was a rebel, a young man who was steeped in patriarchy and hated being slighted, so Kay's family and I were already brewing a volatile scenario. Naturally, and not surprising, I took offense at this demand. I deemed it an unreasonable and highly provocative request.

When Kay's younger sister Julia phoned me reiterating the request that I hand over "our property," as she characterized it, I let her have it, big time. I spouted venom as I belted, "Tell your parents, nothing of the sort is happening. Kay now belongs to the Mafirakureva family and clan. These items you are demanding are matrimonial property, to which you have no claim, so sod off! Your family are objectionable for having the nerve to make this unacceptable request of me!"

"Aaah aaah," the ever-loquacious Julia stammered, struggling for words before I banged the phone down. With any normal family or in-laws, that should have been it, done and dusted, end of, but not with Fugude's family, as I later discovered. In no time, their grasping, slimy, grubby hands would pop up again as they reared their ugly heads. The TV incident should have been my red flag for things to come.

Squabbling and obsessing over money and the perceived financial needs of Fugude's family were to be the centerpiece of my blazing rows with Kay; into that fray the tv incident kept reappearing like a festering wound. Kay made no secret she resented my sending money to Zimbabwe for the upkeep of my widowed mother and my two siblings, Kian, who had just started Journalism school at University of Cape Town, and Kathy, who was commencing her Year 12 at a prestigious all-girls school in Mutare.

"They are not your children," Kay would retort. She'd add, "There's something wrong about you, a child looking out after other children," to which I ejaculated angrily, "Well, I'm afraid, I dis̶a̶g̶r̶e̶e̶. My own father toiled to send me to school, and as a ̶t̶o̶k̶e̶n̶ ̶o̶f̶ acknowledgement and to cherish his memory, I have ̶t̶o̶ ̶l̶o̶o̶k̶ ̶a̶f̶t̶e̶r̶ his wife, my mother, and my two remaining siblings, Kian and Kathy."

̶T̶h̶i̶s̶ ̶i̶n̶f̶u̶r̶i̶a̶t̶e̶d̶ Kay, who was now bristling with anger. "Well, ̶w̶h̶a̶t̶ ̶a̶b̶o̶u̶t̶ ̶m̶e̶ and Alexis?" she yelled at me. "Where do we line up ̶i̶n̶ ̶y̶o̶u̶r̶ plans, seeing as we are not a priority to you in your life?"

"I'm lucky enough to come from a well-to-do background," she continued. "My father is 'Mister Moneybags' himself. He was a big man in his heyday, an estate manager and, thank God, no child in my family has to go through the indignity of looking after another child!

"This is so wrong and unfair, Kundai! And now I see, the children and I are number 10 and 11, and your bloody Zimbabwean family are number one," Kay bellowed, almost hysterical.

These blazing rows over family demands from Zimbabwe became the norm and typified our marriage. Kay liked to emotionally blackmail me over my family's needs, playing what I called a game of numbers, in which she claimed my mother and my two siblings were first, whilst she and the children were on tenth and eleventh position. Of course, nothing was further from the truth, nor as far-fetched as this. It was utterly preposterous of Kay to phrase things this way. Early death had robbed me of an illustrious breadwinner in my father, John Mafirakureva, a hardworking luminary who always did what had to be done providing for the family. I took things personally. I saw her tirades as an attack on me, on my manhood, particularly when she persistently twisted things, insinuating I was not responsible enough in fending for her and the children.

In any case, I found Kay's double standards revolting. Half the time, her mother Fugude was secretly asking for money from Kay, even though Fugude was a primary school teacher in her local Juliusdale community. Fugude loved money excessively, though, which was an attribute Kay inherited from this toxic woman. Many a time in the house, I had come across World Remit and Western Union receipts for huge sums of money dispatched to Fugude, and I had been tactful enough not to ask. This was because I had discovered Kay's deception due to my snooping around in the house, and I didn't want my Sherlock Holmes skills to come back to bite me. Sadly though, what broke my heart was how Kay's mother had managed to drive a permanent wedge of discord amongst her five children and her husband, Walter, the much-touted "big shot," and former estate manager at Aberfoyle Tea Estate in Manicaland. Fugude was a past master of deceit. She was a clever manipulator, not only of her malicious brood of children, but also of her hapless husband, Walter. Fugude could use Walter willy nilly, like when she pulled the puppet strings and Walter unashamedly drove 60 kilometers away to our Vumba homestead and forcibly grabbed the TV from my family.

As if that were not such social opprobrium on his part, Walter had the audacity to come back for the remote control; he forgot it in his haste to leave our homestead. With a cheeky chuckle over the phone, my brother Kian later told me, "As surreal as it appeared, I phoned your father-in-law Walter and alerted him he'd forgot to take the TV remote on his grab jaunt."

"Did he actually drive all the way from Nyanga, just to pick up a remote control?" I asked incredulously.

"Oh yes, he did," Kian replied. "You have to know, *M'koma,* some people have no shame nor a sense of right and wrong, and that is the case with your in-laws, I'm afraid."

And the blazing rows, constant mood swings, and silent treatment from Kay became the hallmark and daily vicissitudes of our now fragile marriage. Meanwhile, Kay's mother was using DHL to send love potions or concoctions from her *Sangomas* / seers; these mixtures were to be used on me so I would become a compliant husband. An avid believer in seers, medicine men and dark mystical forces, Fugude made it her specialty to consult these darker, underworld forces; many a time I had intercepted DHL parcels with these brews and precise instructions to Kay for how to tame me into a pliable husband. Every now and then, Kay would absent-mindedly remark, without any sense of irony, "It is every woman's dream to have a compliant husband." It was as if she said this to justify her faith in the *Sangomas* love potions from her mother. Fugude did not hide it; she had an insatiable appetite for money and all things material. Because she was Kay's mother, she took it upon herself to dictate and interfere in our marriage, her overriding concern being self-interest on her part.

Once, Fugude visited us at our three-bedroom Lay Road house in Aylesbury, and I overhead them plotting and conspiring about how to use African juju on me to ensure I would be the pliable and docile husband Kay so wanted me to be.

"*Haaa haamboteerera mama,* Kundai doesn't listen to me at all as his wife. He would rather take instructions from his mother or sister in Zimbabwe," opined Kay.

"*Haaa tinomugadzira Mafirakureva uyu!* We will fix him with love potions till he plays ball," assured the garrulous Fugude in her uncouth manner.

"Once we are done with him, you'll see you can start sending more money to me. I sent you to school Kay, I expect you to send me lots of money so I can show off and blow my trumpet in Nyanga and Juliusdale, my workplace. Forget about your dad; I should take the credit for raising you. Everyone in Nyanga should look at me in envy, for I am the self-proclaimed queen of swag. I love and revel in attention. Do you know you can be mean, my daughter? Why don't you take a leaf from your North London sister, *sisi* Nyari? That one sends a lot of money to her mother *Maiguru*, and as we speak, she's completed building an imposing mansion for *Maiguru* in Mt. Pleasant Heights. Soon, and very soon, my sister, Mai Nyari, will be living in posh Mt. Pleasant Heights, while I remain ensconced in rural Nyanga, as if my womb didn't give birth," whined Fugude in her manipulative and false self-pitying mode. That was what the woman was good at; she was a master puppeteer, throwing her fingers, pulling the strings, meddling in my marriage to create disharmony and disarray. And then there were their endless shopping trips for clothes. Kay and her mum Fugude, for the duration of her stay with us, and by their shopping jaunts, ensured our spare bedroom was quickly filled and nearly crammed to the ceiling with the duo's penchant for retail therapy. Oft times in the evenings, mother and daughter could be heard giggling on their Aylesbury and North London, Finsbury Park High Street retail therapy conquests of the day.

"Today, I sure gave my credit card a hammering; I shopped till I dropped dead," Kay went on.

"*Aiwa, ndookubaraka uku,* these are the perks and benefits of motherhood. Now I'm getting my pension, whilst I'm still in fulltime employment," cackled Fugude.

"*Mune ndege yenyu mega here* mama, are you going to charter your own little plane to carry all your stuff to Zimbabwe?"

"My son-in-law, Mafirakureva, will pay for any excess baggage arising thereof," Fugude laughed off, much to my squirming discomfort. "After all, he hasn't finished paying off the bride price for you."

That was it, vintage Fugude for you, uncouth in the very extreme, always dredging up any unsavoury details from the sewer. Insulting me, yet she was residing in my house on account of my benevolence. Given my respect to her as my mother-in-law, I tended to ignore these baseless own goals.

Another time, I saw on her phone that Kay was doing WhatsApp consultations on how to tame me with a seer in Zimbabwe, Mbuya Mafuta, the reputable medicine woman from Sakubva township; amongst some of the exchanges were promises by Mbuya Mafuta to courier her herbs via DHL to Kay, as long as Kay paid the courier fees. Upon confronting Kay, I experienced the rough edges of her mouth, as she gave me a severe tongue lashing. I wished I hadn't broached the subject. "Serves you right for snooping into my phone; don't you realize a phone is still an individual, private item, even amongst a married couple? Now, let me clearly tell you what you've done, Kundai, you've clearly breached my confidence and personal space, snooping into my phone like this, and for that, I take great exception. Let me ever catch you again on my phone, I'll give you a good hiding you'll live to remember, if you're lucky to live, that is!" And with that chilling threat of violence, she retired upstairs.

To be fair to Kay, though, my side of the family, friends and colleagues were not entirely blameless in exacting these financial pressure and expectations on us, as we were still trying to settle down in a new habitat called England. In this new land, we discovered a whole new life of constantly working to keep up with speeding household bills. It was always one thing after the other, chasing the household bills, gas, electricity, water, council taxes, you name it. The demands from Zimbabwe refused to acknowledge that I had a separate life now, with a young family to look after.

It is only now, with a bit of perspective and hindsight, that I can see that some of the demands were onerous and stifling to me and my young family with Kay, and perhaps Kay may have had a legitimate point... I don't know.

Random requests for gifts would come from the wider extended family, friends, and former colleagues. I have lost count of the litany of email requests from friends and colleagues from Zimbabwe who wanted a financial bailout from me. I ended up remarking to Kian, "Surely, I am not the governor of the Bank of England, am I?"

"Can we have help with school fees, please, or else your niece, *muzukuru wenyu* will be chucked from school," was one such perennial request.

"*Zvinhu zvaoma muZimbabwe,* i.e., things are increasingly tough and difficult in Zimbabwe; we could do with some help," was another familiar line from home.

"My dad is critically ill. I am calling a favour on you as a trusted friend of many years, to help out with medical fees."

"Whatever small amount you can manage," was also another recurrent motif, with friends from yesteryear.

"I lost my job. Are you still the affable Kundai of old? You have always been a good man. I will come straight to the point, though I am cringing even saying this: I need £5000 from you to pay for my daughter's university tuition in Switzerland," came another request from a friend who had earlier duped me in asking for a loan he never repaid in the end, but he had no shame in coming back.

It hurts me to write about these mercenary motives because these were people I used to hold in high regard as friends and colleagues during my heydays in Mutare, Zimbabwe. And to those who know me well, I'm a stickler for genuine friendship and loyalty. I value loyalty. Some former friends couldn't disguise their mercenary motives. They clearly made it clear to me; they didn't want a friendship relationship anymore, unless money was in the fray. I mourn the loss of such friendships, such as one with a certain Mutisi, a good friend I liked dearly, but he became petulant over an unpaid debt and refuses to speak to me to this day. What a life we live as mere mortals! No wonder the English up north have a saying: There's nought so queer as folk.

Then there were some friends who drifted apart from me because of their insecurities and competitive streak. One such former friend personifies arrogance to high heavens. Nick was so egotistical and self-centred, everything had to be about him and him alone, and how he was doing so well in Zimbabwe. Many a time, unprovoked, he would go on a blistering tirade against those who left Zimbabwe to go and do menial jobs abroad, "cleaning the bottoms of geriatric white people in English care homes," as he put it. The irony of his statements lost on him was that I was one such economic migrant, an economic fugitive in a way. So uncouth was Nick that each time I met him, he would bang on, non-stop, in my face, on how he has eight properties, saying, "I have eight properties, two in South Africa, six in Zim. I am doing well. I don't need to go to England to make it. My UK is in Zimbabwe! You guys have no life out there." Once I took him to see a friend who had just bought a four-bedroom modest house in Milton Keynes, my hood. We were barely out of Ewan's house and Nick was already berating the house for how sub-standard it was with, "My house in Harare is better, plus I've got a large expansive yard, unlike these match boxes you have here."

Nick always had a weird complex within his persona and modus operandi. Perhaps, he was used to treating people like a piece of poo back home, and in his misguided way of thinking and delusions of grandeur, he thought he could do the same here in England. But of course, it didn't work. The last straw which strained our amity was when he recruited me to front for his business interests in England. The deal was, he would use my residential address as his company headquarters' contact address, and I would be a co-director of his company, among other duties.

Always gifted with the gift of the gab and finesse oratory, Nick was a charmer. I remember him persuasively arguing his case to me one afternoon, "Mister Kundai, I have a big, life-changing plan for you, my business proposition. You are going to be a very rich and successful man. In time, you will ditch your teaching career, because of what we are starting now. Global Marketing, PLC." For someone who was getting fed up with the mundane routine of my teaching job, that was sweet music in my ears, but I should have known better. Nick could give you a glowing world in words, but he couldn't walk the talk. I am not saying it was the first time it was happening between him and me. It had happened before, only this time, I had decided to rise above it and give him a second chance. But I should have known better.

As I had come to know Nick quite well, I saw that he liked to use people without paying them and that was ultimately the bone of contention between him and me. After doing much of his leg work, running around to open a UK bank account for him, he was reluctant to pay me for my services, which he tried to downplay as insignificant. Prior to that, he had refused to commit himself to a written contract in relation to my employ with him, going into a rambling, opaque discussion of percentages and how he would first have to deduct a tenth of the wages as my tithe, before he could pay me the difference. I wasn't prepared to be used as a mug and so I emailed him my resignation, which up to this day, has never been formally acknowledged and interaction between us has dwindled. He also took exception when he tried to poach my wife Kay to ditch her secure teaching job so she could become his merchandiser representative. How presumptuous, patronising and insulting of Nick! Kay, being a tough cookie, told him to his face to shove his job, which Nick didn't take kindly, suspecting it was my influence, but, of course, it had nothing to do with me. Kay had her own mind and many a time she'd warned me to be wary of the manipulative streak "of your friend Nick and his wife."

Nick's wife, Jackie was equally shallow, parochial, and very exhibitionist in flaunting their supposed wealth through Instagram and Facebook pictures splashed around. Once, Jacky had unashamedly uploaded fictitious pictures on Facebook, gloating that Nick had bought a small private jet for personal use. It was all false, of course, for some of us, the more astute, who were able to see through this vanity project but chose not to call it out for what it was, lest we were demonised as, "*they are jealous of us and begrudge our wealth and success.*" Yet ironically, it is people like the Nicks of this world who would try to use me to front their so-called businesses in England without remuneration; whenever I questioned these underhanded moves, they went into childish tantrums and threw their toys out of the pram. Later, I had it on good authority from other friends and service providers to whom I had recommended Nick, that settling payments for services rendered appeared to be a problem with him. Interestingly, much as he used to constantly malign England, saying Zimbabwe was his England, when it came to higher education, he ensured his daughters enrolled in English universities. How very telling of human nature!

So, my first few years of settling in England were not only eventful but insightful in revealing the predatory nature of human beings and those people I used to think were my friends. Talk of taxonomy of friendships, or "friends with benefits," as the proverbial saying goes. There are people like that; I've seen them in the short life I've lived. They pigeonhole people according to how useful they can be to them. Beyond that, if anyone is of no material or financial value, they are disposable and of no use to them. Such is life. These are some of the insights I gained, courtesy of my interactions with family, friends, and colleagues. Some excommunicated me completely when they saw their perceived financial benefits were not materialising with me.

They say an apple doesn't fall far from the tree. This insight hits close to home when I reflect on Kay's shenanigans with me and the penny dropped, when in retrospect, I started seeing close similarities between Kay's modus operandi and her mother

Fugude's wily ways. Once, during the early years of our marriage, when I went to Zimbabwe on a visit, I vividly remember Kay seriously exhorting me, "This £200 is for Mama MA," as she called her. "Please don't give it to her in the presence of Papa or when Papa is close by. Papa is controlling and will take all the money from Mama."

What an absolute idiot, to think I fell for such hogwash. Later on, the coin flipped, as I was now on the receiving end of Kay's financial profligacy and deception, which usually manifested in huge debts and household bills not being paid on time, although I was being sold a dummy to the contrary, by Kay. The few moments I sent some money to her Pops Walter, Kay was livid with me, insisting, "Why don't you send it to Mama instead?" Really, it's a weird world when a daughter begrudges her own father being on friendly terms with her husband. But then, the Kay I saw in the later parts of our 13-year marriage was a different Kay, a pale shadow of her former self, increasingly aloof, detached, unkind and unhinged. She was a complete stranger from the woman I married, that young Bonda lassie I fell in love with at St Matthias Tsonzo High School, with her devil's delight cakes she used to bake for me every weekend.

In seeking to apportion blame on what actually unleashed upheaval in my first marriage to Kay, the dissolution of which instigated a chain of events which led to subsequent chaos in my life, I find myself blaming certain aspects of my African culture, particularly the collective sense of expectation for people to be looked after. Looking back, I sometimes find it stifling and overbearing for society and family members, some able-bodied grownups, putting their lives on hold and expecting, *"Aaah m'koma will do it for us; m'koma will look after my family."* I could never fathom why some grown men, like my brothers-in-law, who decided to father their own children, thought it was okay, and my duty to be financially responsible for their children and wives! Surely, once someone decides to sire children, it comes with the territory, right? They should own up and assume responsibility for their kids!

I am still a proponent and custodian of my African culture and Zimbabwean values and identity, but that won't stop me poking holes in parts of my culture with which I have problems, like this sense of obligation by those back home on those of us in the diaspora. Many a time, in response to the constant demands for money or little presents, by family and friends back home, I always ended up saying, "You know what, folks? We all have to carry our own cross; I carry mine; you carry yours. Life goes on." At times, I felt there was a sense and tendency to take me for granted, given the absurdity of some of the requests or demands from the extended family members like my brothers-in-law. You know, as a man, there are some things for which you don't ask help. It just can't be done. There are some things at which a man draws a line. You try to fix your own shit, without involving others. "Play your own drum," as I call it. I washed cars for a living, however demeaning it was during those early days I arrived in England and my wife was off work. It had to be done; that's what being pragmatic entails.

Interestingly, when my life descended into car crash mode following my divorce from Kay, and my disastrous relations with women thereafter, the harshest criticism I got was that I wasn't organised, I'm socially inept, I need to sort myself out, all came from those quarters who were always badgering me for help: friends and family from Zimbabwe! Some of the harshest and cruelest remarks came from those whom I felt had benefitted from my selfless charity. Amongst snippets of remarks, I vividly remember were most eloquently phrased in my Shona vernacular, "*Sekuru havagone kugara nevakadzi.*" Loosely, translated, it was, "Uncle Kundai is a social misfit who can't handle having normal relations with women. His life is a mess and one complete car crash after another."

Some gleefully characterised my misfortunes as a comedy of errors: "The man certainly needs help; pray for him." Of course, it hurt hearing such snide remarks from people whose incessant financial needs and demands catapulted my own life and marriage into the dark abyss, but such is life, I guess. It was exceedingly hurtful this was coming from people I had got along well with, regaling in laughter and gaiety, yet they were twisting the knife in me now. I had considered these people as friends, my kith and kin. They had given me firm handshakes, warm hugs and constantly back slapping me, but all this counted for nothing now from them as they turned their backs on me. So long, life goes on, I silently mumbled to myself giving myself inner resolve. One bizarre occurrence was when my sister's husband, the civil engineer, decided to go after one of my ex's, I mean going after my ex-lover with a whole concoction of lies. How debasing and perverted can one get? But again, I seem to find resonance in the Yorkshire saying my English friend, Naomi Wheeler, shared with me: *"There's nought so queer as folk."* People are weird in what they get up to, and what goes on in their funny little heads.

Meanwhile, as my marital squabbles and bickering with Kay peaked, Zettie came into my life, as a confidante to begin with. Talk of being at the right place, at the right time; I'll give you Zettie for that.

CHAPTER 5

Zettie

I met Zettie Jones at Princes Risborough School (PRS) in Buckinghamshire County where I did my six-weeks placement during my teacher training, and later returned to do some teaching for a few years. Zettie was a stunning looker from the very onset I set my eyes on her. Tall, slim, voluptuous, with pointed nipples for a bosom which always had me unashamedly mesmerized in momentary lapses, caught many atimes in a trance, as I couldn't restrain my lecherous eyes feasting on this beauty. In addition, Zettie had captivating almond blue eyes punctuated by a beautiful, dimpled face with a ravishing smile; it was utterly impossible for anyone to turn their back on her. Time and again, I had come to believe even a monk of the strictest moral code would have been tempted by Zettie's sexual allure, just for one night of sin, if only to have their carnal desires and pleasures quenched by this sublime madonna. On top of that she had a great knack for intelligent conversation, the wildly beautiful lassie could keep you laughing non-stop with her stories and friendly banter. She certainly made an impression on me, with her long blond hair loosely hanging on her shoulders. We hit it off straightaway, as friends that is. Zettie was a young, wild, free spirit, a liberal-minded, young, white girl from an affluent Buckinghamshire family, who was very much fascinated by many things about me, not least of which was my heavy Zimbabwean accent. And she constantly badgered me on how she wanted to learn about Zimbabwean culture, history, and identity and I should take her to Zimbabwe so she could immerse herself in our way of life.

"Tell me about Zimbabwe, Kundai, I mean what is life like over there? Is it all the doom and gloom as we see in the news and media channels?" Zettie would ask.

"Far from it Zet, apart from the tragic failure of leadership, Zim is a beautiful country endowed with picturesque landscapes and cityscapes, not to mention my fellow citizens and their sense of ubuntu."

"Really?"

"Of course, you will love and appreciate many things about my country, Zet, as long as we take the politics out of the fray. We have the majestic Vumba Mountains, where we happen to have our family homestead. Then there is beautiful Mutare, where I grew up and went to school. I haven't even mentioned the sprawling cities, Harare and Bulawayo, the latter boasting of Matopos Hill, among other sterling locations. I'm sure you've also heard of the much-touted Victoria Falls, one of the much-eulogized wonders of the world."

Saying this usually made Zet squeal in unmitigated delight, "Oh you really ought to invite me to witness these splendours, mate!"

"Of course, I will," I remarked with a cheeky wink at her. "Now, here is a bit about my family, Zet. We are the *Mafirakureva* clan, we originally hail from Vumba, famed for its beautiful, mountainous terrain and ever-green fauna, ensconced in the eastern part of Zimbabwe, bordering Mozambique. Our totem is *Gwai, Gumbi, Mukuruvambwa*. *Mukuruvambwa*, a Shona term meaning one has to conduct themselves like a proper grown up in order to earn the respect of the youngsters, which is something very typical of my family elders. I've seen from my kith and kin that they conduct themselves with effortless grace and modesty. I have to tell you, the *Mafirakureva* clan… we are a distinguished family in Zimbabwe." There was so much pride and adulation in my voice, especially in extoling the virtues of my family to Zettie.

"What's a totem?" asked an increasingly befuddled-looking Zettie. I could see she was completely mystified by this seemingly rambling, totem talk.

I remarked with a mischievous grin on my face, "Well, you said you wanted to learn about our Zim culture, didn't you? A totem is something unique to every Zimbabwean family; you could say, it's a kind of mystical, cultural practice or belief, whereby an individual family refrains from eating a certain animal's meat as a mark of reverence, and in our family's case, we do not eat any sheep meat at all."

"But why wouldn't you?" Zettie remarked incredulously. "You poor thing. Roast lamb is among some of the most succulent dishes anyone can ever have, and you're telling me it's a no-go area for you?"

"I'm afraid, yes, that's the correct position, Zet, or else…"

"What do you mean, "or else?"

"Well, here is the thing, Zet, if anyone from my clan, both immediate and extended family members, dare eat lamb, then there are cultural reprisals like, one's front teeth just fall off as a sanction from the ancestors for not respecting family cultural values. I've seen this first-hand amongst my fathers' six sisters, *wana Tete*. They all have missing front teeth. And my father used to reprimand us when we were young, using his errant sisters as a deterrent.

"'They disrespected the family through eating sheep meat, and now look what happened to their front teeth! All gone,'" Dad would say, shaking his head in utter disgust and exasperation at this perceived transgression.

I am not sure Zettie was entirely convinced by my rationale and correlation behind my aunties losing their front teeth over some opaque cultural transgressions, but if she had any doubts, out of respect for my cultural beliefs, she kept her skepticism to herself, though her body language betrayed her misgivings.

At the time of our meeting, June 2005, it was unthinkable anything like a relationship would ever occur between Zettie and me. I was still with Kay, albeit the cracks having started. Zettie had just completed her PGCE at Oxford Brookes University and had this philandering boyfriend she was trying to shake off, "Jake the lad," as she called him.

In time, Zettie and I became increasingly close. I remember, the first day after our meeting at PRS, one summer in July, Zettie drove me home in her small Ford Fiesta. Wow, that blew me away! A fine looking, young Englishwoman, taking time out for me for the 20-minute drive to Aylesbury from Princes Risborough village. It turns out, as time progressed, with Zettie's on/off relationship with Jake hitting the brick wall, and my mounting marital woes with Kay, Zettie and I naturally gravitated towards each other. As clichéd as it sounds, in the words of Hot Chocolate's renowned classic, *It started with a kiss* at Zettie's parents' house, a sprawling country estate in the picturesque Chilten Mountains of Buckinghamshire. Zet came onto me, full steam ahead, which was exciting and alluring in a way. "It's your birthday, Kundai, are you not even going to let me kiss you?" she said, cheekily blushing at me. And so, it happened; on my 32nd birthday I crossed the line and started cheating on my wife, Kay. What Jada Pinkett Smith popularized as *entanglement* commenced between Zettie and me, as we both became entangled.

That birthday night we did it, marathon style, with Zettie moaning and swooning all over my hairy chest. I knew I was pleasing her, when I heard her purring with unmitigated pleasure as I softly rubbed my fingers between her wet, receptive thighs. I could feel her clitoris erect and tantalizingly inviting. Now, I was on solid ground with her, as she cried for it relentlessly and I rammed my stiff cock into her, thrusting in-out-in-out with reckless abandon, much to her delight as her fingernails dug into me in a wild frenzy of euphoric ecstasy. Our bodies exploded into a surreal orgasm which gave us tingling sensations. After what seemed like an eternity, we were both spent and had that contented glow which comes from mind blowing sex.

She was certainly a vixen in bed, no two ways about it! Our birthday nooky was to mark the genesis of many meetups to occur between us. That was the turning point in our relationship as we quickly transitioned from friends to amorous lovers. The night provided a cloak of discretion over our shady nocturnal activities. Zettie had beauty and brains, such a potent combination which I found more sexually alluring and something of an aphrodisiac. Many atimes, I reaped the rewards of her beautiful, lithe body, constantly thrusting in and out of her inner crevices with wild abandon which gave both of us multiple orgasms.

Looking back, there was no way my marriage to Kay would have survived in the face of these constant sexual trysts with Zettie. The fact that Zettie was white made it all the more intriguing for me, coming from a culture which tended to "worship" and eulogize whiteness. Each time I entered her, and upon coming, I felt like I was getting back at the British colonial master for "raping" Mama Africa's continent. So shagging Zettie was more like Britain's comeuppance, which certainly acted as an aphrodisiac to keep me going, long, full steam ahead. At least, that seemed to make sense in my own little head.

And so, it happened one summer holiday. I flew to Zimbabwe with Zettie, which is how she first met my kid brother Kian, who was later to join us in England. Being a people person, classy and sassy, Zet appeared to have hit it off straightaway with Kian, as they both sat long drawn-out hours on the veranda at our Vumba homestead in Mutare, downing lagers and continuously chain smoking weed, as if they had known each other for ages. That summer holiday, it was constant giggles between Zettie and Kian. I had no suspicions then. How could I have? In my mind, these were two friendly people close to me, and the fact that they jelled was fine by me. Had I not always banged on about Kay being anti-my family? What better way was there, than having a consort who gets along well with your family like Zet did? I was actually excited; Zet was front footed on this one. To cap it all, my sister Kathy also warmed up to Zet and was effusive in eulogizing her. *"Aaah akasununguka chaizvo,* she is the ideal *muroora,* daughter-in-law we never had. It's been humbling and fulfilling interacting with her; she's so down to earth for a white woman, coming here and embracing us, our culture and way of life here, just like that, with no airs," gushed Kathy, much to my innermost delight and smiles. I was secretly chuffed, none of the family members had disparaged my new female friend or censured me for bringing her home, as I was still, on paper, married to Kay. *Perhaps their non-criticism of me is a sign of tacit approval,* I rationalised within myself.

We returned to England and life returned to its normal routine of Zettie and me with our hectic professional lives as English teachers. As my relationship with Zet blossomed, there were murmurs of disapproval from some within the staff grapevine community, who somehow had sussed out that I was playing the field, as I had a live-in wife. The more daring among them tried to warn off Zet. She told them to bugger off. That was my Zet, always fearfully defensive over me, over us. Once the head teacher called Zet in for a private meeting, as he found it disturbing that Zet was having a relationship with me, another member of staff, and Zet gave it back to Rowan Sharper, the school head, "But excuse me Rowan, I'm sorry, I don't really get this. What's your problem? Kundai and I having a relationship?" To which Rowan responded, "I'm afraid we have a duty to set standards for the children, standards for the community, especially where it comes to potentially married men..." Zet tells me she never got to let him finish his statement, but firmly put Rowan in his place, saying, "With all due respect, Rowan, I'm afraid you've over-stepped your brief here. Do you have a problem with Kundai's ethnicity, or what? Since when do head teachers become marriage counsellors? What about other members of staff at this school in relationships like me and Kundai? Do you also call them for a tete-a-tate?"

I'm told Rowan was dumbfounded by Zet's blasé attitude and mumbled, "I'm only trying to play my pastoral role as your Head," which further infuriated Zet, and she responded, "Unless my relationship with Kuu is jeopardizing my job, I don't really see how this is any of your concern, Rowan, and if you can excuse me please." Zet tells me that's how the frosty meeting ended between her and the Head Rowan, after which she defiantly walked out, her voluptuous hips swaying. "This is cause for celebration, honey," I remarked, and that weekend we had a quiet get away in London.

Free spirit that Zet was, from that incident on, she tried to make it exceedingly obvious we were in a relationship, especially with her public displays of affection. Her defense to me was, "Well, honey, we are adults and can damn well do as we please, as long as we are not hurting anyone." It was weird to me that Zet said this, as I'm sure Kay would have argued we were hurting her with our cheating game. Zet told me, "Well, Kuu, like I said to Rowan, unless fucking you is impeding my job as an English teacher, then, yes, I would give Rowan an audience," to which we both laughed at the absurdity of it.

Meanwhile, as I consolidated my relationship with Zet, I was still living with Kay, who was blissfully unaware of my Nikodemus shenanigans with Zettie. But our rowing had now escalated up a notch further. If it wasn't screaming matches from Kay, she was giving me the silent treatment, which was something I really struggled to deal with. Perhaps Kay had a split personality, as it later dawned with time. I will always marvel at how she could give me the silent treatment for weeks on end, and kept me in the doghouse, but if the phone rang, she would instantly jump on it, chatting animatedly with her friends, like Lucy, talking nonchalantly as if things were normal in her life. But if I tried to initiate conversation after the phone calls, all I got were evils and not a word from her.

CHAPTER 6

The Centre Can No Longer Hold

And even as our bickering with Kay encroached onto our marital bed, I knew the end was nigh. Everything with Kay had to be framed within an argument of some sort. We were always haggling and bargaining, like it was some commercial transaction. Really? Begging for sex from your wife? I remember Kay's aunt, who had come to mediate in one of our endless squabbles, earnestly admonishing her niece Kay in our vernacular, "*Mu bedroom hamusi mucourt, hamutongwi nyaya muzukuru,*" which, literally translated, is, "the marital bed is sacrosanct, a place for lovers to consummate their love and not raise squabbles or try to settle scores with your husband, my dear niece." Sadly, Tete's wise counsel fell on deaf ears, as my sex life with Kay was governed and conducted according to her manipulative terms, when she wanted it, when it suited her. Once my brother Sam came from Coventry to visit us for a weekend with his wife Miranda, and I stayed up very late, until everyone had gone to bed, so I could sneak into the spare bedroom to sleep, because I didn't want them to notice I was no longer sharing the matrimonial bed with Kay. I felt embarrassed about this ever coming out, but I need not have wasted my time with the sneaking around and stealth. Both Sam and Miranda later jokingly told me they had clearly sussed it out that Kay and I were not sleeping together, despite my attempts at fooling them. What a world we live in.

Where I lacked in intimacy at home, Zettie was my medicine, giving it to me in leaps and bounds, with boundless zeal and energy. I am not justifying my infidelity, but good old Zettie was there for me when I needed comfort most. Strange how we grow up, morally upright and all prim and proper, adhering to a strict moralistic code, and yet here I was, a well-brought up Salvation Army Sunday school lad, having an enjoyable entanglement with my concubine Zettie, banging her at will; quite a far cry from Kay's preconditional negotiations to go through before sex. There was this weekend when Zettie organised a getaway for us to Wales, picturesque Wales, where we retreated to the Cardiff beach, residing in a self-catering cottage. By day we explored the rugged, mountainous terrain of Abergavenny town and outskirts, which in a way reminded me of my hometown, Mutare, Zimbabwe.

Whatever her transgressions with Kian, Zettie showed me love and unmitigated passion. One minute we could be in gaggles of laughter regaling together over her limitless wit and riddles. "So, what do you call a thousand lawyers chained together at the bottom of the ocean? Go on, make sense of my riddle," teased Zet, looking at me cheekily.

"But I don't get it," I said sheepishly to her.

"Dummy, try harder, Andy," for that was Zettie's pet name for me.

"But I can't," I shot back at her, "Give me a better clue."

"Okay, let me be generous then," went on Zet, "Aaah, think lawyers, and your dislike of lawyers."

I still couldn't crack her riddle and admitted, "Oh, okay, I give up, Zet. Help me out." I resigned in frustration, shrugging my shoulders, lifting my hands high.

"Andrew!" for that was Zet's best way to annoy me. She knew I hated that name, my middle name. "Dummy Andrew, remember *Philadelphia*, your favourite film? And in the moving scene, when Denzel Washington visits his client Tom Hanks in hospital to congratulate him on his legal victory?"

"Oh yes, I remember," I brightened up now, but still, I could not get the joke. "Zet, go on, take me out of my misery and I promise you a treat tonight," I pleaded.

"Okay, bumbling idiot, it's a lawyer joke and you know how you are always banging on about your general loathing and dislike of grubby, grasping lawyers, and how all they do is line their pockets. Well, it's a straightforward joke, like in *Philadelphia*, a thousand lawyers chained together at the bottom of the sea would be, one good starting point!" Zet remarked, flashing her dazzling smile at me.

It was at that point I started laughing, as the penny dropped. "A thousand lawyers chained at the bottom of the ocean! What a twisted fuck you are, Zet!"

Later, in the course of my acrimonious divorce with Kay, I was to constantly replay this joke in my head when her solicitors gave me a torrid time with trumped up charges of domestic violence against Kay, clearly meant to soil my reputation and prevent contact with my children. So Zet was right after all, a thousand lawyers chained together at the bottom of the sea would be one good starting point in getting rid of unscrupulous lawyers.

Following the Wales getaway weekend, returning home to grumpy old Kay was surreal. I still lived with Kay in the midst of my trysts and entanglements with Zet, possibly because of my guilt at wanting to still see the children. Talk of having one's cake and eating it at the same time. Kay was in a foul mood immediately I entered the living room; she was spoiling for a fight. "Where were you this entire weekend? Your phone was unreachable," she barked at me aggressively.

"I had a problem with my phone," I answered her politely.

It appeared to rile her, and then she went for me big time, guns blazing. "So, you think I'm an idiot and don't realise I'm aware of your white whore affair?" she charged.

"White whore?" I tried to play the innocent card.

"Don't you dare give me that bullshit, Kundai," Kay bellowed, charging at me like an enraged elephant. I had to make a quick dive out of the way. "Today, I'll give it to you, after which you'll leave for your stinking white whore!" As she spoke, she was shoving my clothes in black bin bags, which she angrily threw out of the house. Calming Kay was out of the question, as it only further incensed her. That Sunday evening marked the first time Kay evicted me from the matrimonial home, and I went to live with Zet for some time.

Zettie was a smart woman who played her cards well. So switched on was she, that she went out of her way to learn more about traditional Zimbabwean dishes and culture, such that she could cook my favourite Zimbabwean dishes like *sadza* and *maguru*, cow intestines and tripe, which she did very well. And she could serve it with a playful banter, and a curtsy of her body. "All yours, *Gumbi*," she'd say, referring to my clansmen's family totem. Honestly, hearing just that alone would give me a hard on. Zet knew how to get the best out of me.

Once, I playfully asked her, "What's your secret recipe Zet? You're such a wonderful blessing to me, love? I'm so lucky to have you."

"There are two ways to a man's heart Kundai," Zet would say.

"And what are those?" I would earnestly enquire.

She would remark, with a straight face, "A daily dose of an empty scrotum and ensuring his belly is well fed," to which I bellowed into guffaws of laughter at her wit.

"Well, Zet," I replied cheekily, amid my mirthful laughter and chuckles. "I'm sure, the way to a woman's heart is to keep her bottom wet all the time, and her cheeks dry."

"Oh yes, I'm up for that," chuckled Zet, winking at me.

We had something great between us, Zettie and I. We hardly

rowed. Our lovers' tiffs were often fairly limited and, in any case, were usually mitigated by the good sex we both enjoyed. Perhaps this consolidated the bond between us. Making love to Zet was like being eaten alive by a wolf, only this was a nicer kind of wolf, which left me wretched and panting for more. We had such a vibrant relationship going, my heart constricted then at the thought of ever losing Zet. I loved her dearly with every nerve in my body. I craved her like she was a drug especially given our wild shenanigans in bed. The sex between us was always explosive. Zet was tireless in bed, full of boundless energy and creativity.

Our similar appreciation of music and Zet's adaptability also helped in bonding us further. I would say we were good friends. We went to the Glastonbury Music Festival in 2017. What a blast we had, savouring the headline acts: Radiohead, Foo Fighters and Ed Sheeran, amongst a talented global line up, a who's who of royalty in music. Much to our delight, the Bee Gees legend, Barry Gibb, performed in the iconic Legend's slot. "Oh my, oh my," Zet and I would remark years later. "Barry nailed it that afternoon. What a sublime performance!" Then Labour Leader Jeremy Corbyn, or Jezza, as we affectionately called him, happened to be there also, and when he gave a rousing speech on the famous Pyramid Stage, Zet and I, like the crowd, went into a wild frenzy, singing along with the crowd, "Oh, Jeremy Corbyn, Oh Jeremy Corbyn!"

I have so many pleasant memories of Zet. Perhaps, I'm a simp, as I still love her dearly, I think.

Among a plethora of functions, we'd attended think tanks, public fora, and Black Lives Matter Movement protests in London together, and Zet would argue passionately, "How you lot have been disadvantaged by the tide of history from time immemorial!" It was not patronising or said condescendingly by Zet, because she spoke from the heart. There was a unique candour and genuineness about her. I could see it from her demeanour.

Whenever cases of social injustice were palpable, she was in top form, she became fired up, always. "We root for the underdog Kuu, social justice is the article of my faith and convictions," she would often remark. "It's a quintessential British trait, to side with the downtrodden, Kuu."

"I know Zet," I remarked, smiling, patting her forehead. I needed no convincing, I knew Zet was sincere in terms of how she felt about race relations, social justice and civil rights matters. I remember vividly how she'd been visibly pained by the passing on of respected civil rights icon John Lewis and Ruth Bader Ginsburg, US Supreme Court Justice, whom Zet characterised as "the rock star of the legal profession." As testament to her enduring adulation, Zet wrote a glowing eulogy for both luminaries, which went on to be published in both *The Guardian* and the *New York Times*. I was touched by this gesture of Zet's.

"Well done, you, Zet. I'm immensely proud of you," I remarked, back slapping her on the shoulders and all choked up over her glowing articles on two icons I also deeply venerated. Our genuine desire and love for a just world was one key area where the glue of our relationship coalesced. Many times, we had vibrant exchanges in which we both shared our frustrations with what Zet termed, the rise of the "dark economies," and what I called "Right-wing Populism."

To my thinking, it was all too palpable how Zet had stuck her neck out for me over her family, particularly her mother, who felt "uncomfortable" her daughter was dating a black man. "I have to warn you Kuu, my parents are not so enlightened. Perhaps I'm being unfair to give such a blanket generalisation by grouping them both, as it's mostly Mum, good old Sophie, but I've put her in her place and firmly told her, 'I'm sticking with my tall, dark and handsome Kuu, my choice, not yours, so live with it!' Dad is all right, really, so let me rephrase my earlier statement, as it's mostly Sophie who has a problem with me dating you." But even Sophie's race-tinged misgivings were not strong enough to torpedo our relationship.

CHAPTER 7

Arise Baby Edmund - Squaring the Circle

One evening, six weeks after our Zimbabwe trip, Zet had some wonderful news to share with me. "Close your eyes, Kuu, she said. "I have something special to share with you."

"What is it," I asked, looking at her askance.

"Well, let's just say, you'll love it," Zet persisted.

"Okay, go on then, bring it on," I egged her on.

"Ready, are you?" Zet said, placing something which felt like plastic in my hands. "You can open your eyes now, sweetie," she remarked, at which point, I saw myself looking at ultrasound images.

"What is this?" I enquired, increasingly bewildered, to a Zet who was the only one seemingly enjoying and savouring the scene.

"Well, I've been keeping this quiet, just so I wouldn't raise your hopes then dash them again. Since our return from Zimbabwe, I started experiencing morning sickness, something quite out of the ordinary for me," Zet went on. "Last week I had a pregnancy test, which proved inconclusive, and so this morning I went to the doctors, they did a pregnancy scan, and took some blood samples, therein, in your hands are the ultrasound photographs showing I'm six weeks and two days pregnant."

"Aaah, I see. Congratulations, Zet," I said. I felt a bit overwhelmed, not knowing exactly what to say, as so many other thoughts were coursing through my mind, not least of which was Kay's reaction if she knew I had a child out of wedlock. Not that it mattered; our marriage had irretrievably broken down and was only subsisting on paper now.

"You don't at all seem pleased," chided Zet. "Don't you want it?"

"Of course, I do, you know I do, Zet," I said reassuringly, stroking her forehead. "When is the expected delivery date?" I enquired.

"It's on the accompanying letter, early Spring, 22nd of May, the letter says."

"Hmmm, so come May, you and I will be proud parents!" I quipped.

News of the imminent baby brought an added impetus and new dynamic to my relationship with Zet. Inwardly, I started flirting with the idea of finally calling time on my dysfunctional marriage with Kay. I did not see us going any further, especially now, with a baby on the way. So, I visited a solicitor, Kathy Lamont, who advised me accordingly, and I filed for divorce proceedings. That decision was just the genesis of my troubles and would cost me dearly, both emotionally and financially, as Kay went into full-scale, virulent, vindictive mode, lashing out at me venomously.

Kay kick-started her war of attrition by chucking my clothes and belongings out of the matrimonial home, after which she alerted me with a text message. I promptly drove to Aylesbury and quite a spectacle greeted me outside 5 Lay Road. Much like a litany, a procession of my clothes was strewn all over the garden lawn and pavement, including my books and paper files. My MacBook Pro was also on the grass.

"Hello Kay," I said, trying to engage her in a conversation, hoping I would be able to thaw the febrile atmosphere and we could have an adult conversation, but Kay was a loose cannon.

"I'm not having anything to do with you, Kundai, you've filed for divorce, and as far as I'm concerned, it means you don't want to live here anymore. So, I've saved you the hassle. Get your ass out of my sight," Kay bawled at me. I knew I wasn't going to make any headway with Kay that evening.

It was clear the divorce petition had rattled her by tipping her over the edge. She appeared to be increasingly unhinged, as she was still throwing some of my clothes in black bin bags, amid hurling obscenities and expletives at me. Years later, I've had a chance to reflect on why she went berserk on a night she should have been able to accept what had long become a drawn-out formality, a failed marriage. It had come to its logical conclusion; why not like it or lump it? I have never really understood that bit of Kay. Perhaps it was part of her split, bipolar disorder, which was the hallmark of her mostly irrational behaviour throughout our marriage.

I still wanted to get into the matrimonial home to check that I had all my personal belongings, but given Kay's aggressive streak, with her foaming and frothing through the ears and mouth, it was unmistakable that getting into the house that night was unlikely. It was then that I did what any law-abiding citizen would do: I called on the local police to offer me practical assistance to ensure I could gain entry to the house. They, however, were not remotely interested at all. "If your wife says she doesn't want you in the house, then you're better off doing her bidding," came the police officer's voice over the phone, before he continued, "You are better off looking for accommodation somewhere else for tonight and the next few days, until your wife cools down."

"But I have nowhere to go," I remonstrated with the officer, still over the phone.

The officer returned, "Go to a friend's house or a hotel. You're actually lucky we are telling you this. If you attempt to enter your house without your partner's consent, we will come and arrest you."

"Arrest me for what!" I shot back at the officer. "Are you equally aware this is my house, as well as Kay's? I am paying the mortgage on this house." I sounded matter of factly with this last declaration, but the police officer wasn't at all fazed and remained defiant. I would spend the night in a police cell if I went ahead bulldozing my way into the house.

I know when I'm beaten. I politely put down the phone, after first enquiring of the officer his name and force number and informing him I was going to cross-check his advice with my legal counsel, first thing Monday morning, as it happened to be a weekend. This was to be the first of my many unsavoury encounters with Thames Valley police officers, in which I would remain increasingly dissatisfied and be on the receiving end of their biased service against black males in domestic dispute incidents. Following this tetchy phone call, I drove back to the wonderful bosom of my dearest Zettie. Inwardly, I felt ready and prepared to cross the Rubicon with Kay.

CHAPTER 8

The Lost Years

Following the split from Kay, it took two complete years of my life in which I didn't get to see our children, Alexis and Brooklyn. Kay went into full-galore, vindictive, spiteful mode, deliberately preventing me from seeing the children, although I had successfully fought in court for the right, singlehandedly representing myself against all odds. Kay had state appointed lawyers, one of whom I nicknamed "the Rottweiler," because he used to growl during court proceedings, as if to intimidate and cow me into silence. He had protruding yellow teeth and that made him look more menacing. The productive time I could have had with my children was lost in protracted legal battles, mostly instigated by Kay to frustrate me. Possibly, she hoped I would give up my dream to have a meaningful relationship with the children. Once, she threatened to change the children's surnames to her maiden surname, and this filled me with dread.

Among her flurry of false allegations against me were claims that I was inherently violent and couldn't be trusted to be with the children. Throughout court proceedings, Kay cynically enjoyed playing the victim and weaponizing non-existent trauma she'd suffered during the marriage, in order to give credence to her false narrative. Of course, the irony was lost on her that as a serving schoolteacher, I had to undergo periodic enhanced criminal disclosure checks which would have revealed or laid bare her accusations. So, as a follow up to her allegations, she decreed I had to see the children at a contact centre between 9am and 12:30pm every other Saturday, since I couldn't be trusted to be alone with my children. The district judge gave the green light to this.

Nothing hurt me so much as these patent falsehoods from Kay, a woman I had lived with for 13 years, and who surely knew the true nature of my inner personality, far removed from her fanciful concoctions. I have to commend The Brackley School's Headteacher, Simon Reece; not only did he allow me to attend all the protracted court appearances, but also wrote on my behalf an excellent character reference for submission to court, attesting to my integrity and rapport with children and how it would be a travesty to deny me the chance to see my own biological children so I could cultivate a relationship and bond with them. One day, when my time is up, in my valedictory speech I will acknowledge and thank the school for their support of me during a darker period in my life, the divorce.

As a devoted father, keen to see my children and forge a relationship with both Alexis and Brooklyn, I reluctantly agreed to Kay's contact centre madness. The first day of this supervised contact visit was steeped in melodrama, typical only of Kay's malevolent, manipulative streak and silly mind games. Kay through the over officious contact centre woman had some do's and don'ts for me, which the woman read out like a prison warden's roll call, i.e.: I was not allowed to take any pictures of my own children, neither should I attempt to give them any presents. And she saved the worst news for the last; according to her, Alexis was in the building in a flood of tears because she didn't want to see me. Fed up with Kay's puerile mind games, I replied, through the annoying contact centre woman, "If Alexis doesn't want to see me, then so be it. That's fine, that's her own choice, she's made her own choice, so it will be respected. Good morning," and I walked away to the other part of the building to have fun with Brooklyn. I was determined enough to thumb my nose at Kay's military style regimental instructions, which I did by taking pictures of Brooklyn with my iPad, much to the contact centre woman's chagrin.

"Excuse me, but you're not allowed to take pictures of the children, or to take out your iPad," she barked at me menacingly. I gave it back in equal measure, "Aaah, sorry to offend you ma'am, I didn't realize it's now a criminal offence in England to take pictures of one's children, and that I need permission for this."

"If you are going to be sassy with me, then I will have you removed from the building; your ex-wife clearly said no pictures and presents, and we have to respect her wishes," the woman affirmed.

I looked at the contact centre woman disdainfully and reflected upon the irony of her words, which she was somehow missing. Here was another woman, preventing another parent from having a relationship with their child, and yet in the same breath, was pontificating about upholding rights for the other party, a vindictive parent. Such revolting hypocrisy! *Surely, one couldn't make up this stuff. Where are the rights of the father then?* I pondered to myself.

Later, in subsequent court proceedings, Kay was to reiterate before a district judge that Alexis didn't want to see me and that was why Kay was obstructing contact. The flip side of these lies by Kay was that they were later disputed by Alexis herself, when increasingly, after her sixteenth birthday, she started having discreet contact with me by phone and email as, "Mummy doesn't want me to talk with you."

Bitterness is a sign of failed humanity. I learnt to reflect on Kay's unwarranted war of attrition against me, seeking to spitefully punish me for daring to end an unproductive marriage. I saw the lowest of the low, highlighted through mostly underhand, sadistic behaviour employed by Kay, whose sole purpose was designed and aimed at hurting me. But perhaps things always came back to a pre-ordained nexus for Kay: power retention. Everything was a power trip with Kay, from sex and even in a normal conversation, she had to have the last word. Obsession with manic power and the need to be in control resided in Kay's very bosom, and sadly, that also spelt troubles for her.

Up to now, I am convinced something wasn't right with Kay for her to harbour such negative energy. Could it be she never forgave me for instigating the divorce? But surely, even the hardest of hearts heals and people learn to move on. Oftentimes, I couldn't help reflecting and drawing analogies with Nelson Mandela's astute observation on how forgiveness is a powerful force which liberates the soul, and if we carry on, mired in bitterness, then we end up prisoners, ourselves.

In a separate occasion, when Kay further accused me of having been violent during the course of the marriage, the district judge considered these as very serious allegations and ordered a full disclosure from the police against my name. This came back as negative, a clear vindication of me, but then wily Kay still had another trick up her sleeve. She told the bemused district judge that the reason there was no corroborating evidence from the police was because, in our Zimbabwean culture, it's perfectly acceptable for men to hit their women or wives and "much as Kundai used to physically abuse me, I didn't report it to the police because it is part of my culture to accept it and get on with it as part of marriage."

I was aghast, visibly shaken, and upset by these gross misrepresentations of our beloved culture. More so, I felt aggrieved she was fomenting and feeding anachronistic stereotypes about my race to white people in positions of authority, thus undermining their perception of black people. I felt insulted on behalf of my fellow citizens, to have them racially profiled like this by one of their very own. I demanded an apology and retraction from Kay, following the vindication from the police about my character. In typical Kay fashion, the apology was not forthcoming; predictably, the district judge encouraged me to move on, for the sake of progress with the case. Then, at the start of court proceedings, Kay came to court with a friend of hers, purportedly to offer her support. The friend, a certain Lucy, also known as Mai Tawanda, tried to gate-crash into the district judge's private chambers, but was fortunately denied entry.

We certainly live in a weird world where people can be grossly misguided to think they can tinker with the justice system at will. *This is England, not some banana republic,* I mused. In retrospect, I have tried to rationalise why Kay's friend Lucy felt duty bound to attend a private family court session. I can only think, perhaps she also wanted to hammer the last nail into my proverbial coffin in this bitter legal wrangling with her friend. Part of me also reflected, I had bumped into Lucy at the Glastonbury Music Festival, when I was with Zet. Now it made sense how Kay may have ended up knowing about what I, all along, thought was my clandestine relationship with Zet. Whatever her motives and misguided sense of loyalty, I'm glad Lucy was denied entry to a private, bruising encounter in which I felt I needed all the privacy in the world.

Throughout the lengthy court proceedings, Kay increasingly became a caricature, all in a bid to spite me and drive a wedge between the children and myself. In one instance, she pointed out to the presiding judge, "It's pointless to allow him to see the children, as they don't like him; they don't' want to see him either." As the district judge who presided over our case was a woman, Kay erroneously thought she could invoke notions of universal sisterhood to her advantage. On one occasion, Kay openly requested to speak with the judge privately in her chambers, to which the judge took exception and firmly declined, after which she censured Kay heavily, putting her in her rightful place. Goodness knows the multitude of times Kay persistently infringed upon the court-sanctioned orders, particularly child contact orders, but still managed to get away with it, thumbing her nose at the justice system.

There was a time I started flirting with the idea of joining the radical, "militant" group, Fathers4Justice, a sign of my utter frustration and sense of despair at failing to see the children, even though I had so many court orders at my disposal. Many a time, I turned up at the Lay Road doorstep to see my children on the designated Saturday, and Kay would simply make them unavailable. Thames Valley Police were persistently unhelpful whenever I called on them for help, as they always seemed to read from a prepared script: "It's a domestic incident. We can't intervene. You have to go back to court to seek redress." Go back to court, my word. I made count of the 11 times I went to court, and each time Kay did not show, yet she continued to draw monthly child maintenance payments from me for the very children she did not want me to see.

How morally repugnant is this! At times Kay would send me a text message at six in the morning on the day I was meant to pick up the kids, and unilaterally cancel my visitation rights, just like that, at the drop of a hat, "because the kids have a tummy bug," or "they don't want to see you." These were some of Kay's default vindictive positions to get back at me. And in my mind, I noted the biased nature of our justice system against fathers. I quietly reflected, *were these not the same police officers who had threatened to apprehend me if I tried to get in my own house, when Kay had evicted me, and yet they can't help me now to respect a court order which allows me to see my children?*

The police said they couldn't help me because it's a domestic incident. How twisted is this? Are they not custodians of the law, which they are supposed to uphold? You are prepared to arrest a man for wanting to get into his house, for which he dutifully pays a mortgage, just because his vindictive wife doesn't want him to get in the house. Hear me out clearly here: the man is not threatening any violence. He just wants entry into his house, but you will not hear of that; you are on the side of the "wronged woman." And yet, when the same woman flouts court orders, you are not prepared to sanction her, "because it's a domestic incident, we can't get involved." That was my experience at the hands of Thames Valley Police Force. I will not even put race into it, but thanks to the Black Lives Matter Movement, certain injustices within the establishment are becoming increasingly clear. Institutionalised racism within the Metropolitan Police force, for instance, is a matter of public record, even from serving and retired police officers.

And so, it came to pass on the 11th occasion I attended family court and Kay was predictably not in court again, I decided to throw in the towel, and the first thing I said to the woman judge was to promptly inform her, "Sorry ma'am, but I am now withdrawing the case," to which she enquired why. And I responded with my treatise, "I give up. She has won. My ex-wife can keep the children for all she wants and prevent contact as she's been doing. She has won. I have come here for the past ten consecutive occasions; she doesn't turn up, and you don't do anything to her. There are pre-existing court orders which she continues to flout with impunity, so yes, it's been a long-drawn-out war of attrition, and to give myself sanity, let me withdraw the case."

The district judge was pensive as she looked at me intently and responded to my mini-speech, "Firstly, Mr. Mafirakureva, I am sorry you feel let down by us, and I sincerely apologize for our shortcomings. We have let you down as the justice system, but if you will just allow me to do one other extra thing, we can still sort something out for you, and you can be able to see your children." The judge went on to say, "And after I've done what I intend to do, then yes, it's within your rights, you can withdraw the case if you still want to."

To which I said, "What else could you possibly do which can make her respect court dates and appearances, which hasn't been done before? She has flouted community orders," to which the Judge calmly replied, "Well, I can arrest her, and make her to be brought to court. The court has very wide powers and discretion at its disposal, which it can use in these matters."

I went quiet for a good few minutes, inwardly ruminating on what the judge had said. I clearly didn't want Kay to be arrested, as I knew this would have a detrimental effect on the kids, so, I made my thoughts known to the judge, "I'm sorry, but I don't want my ex-wife to be arrested, as that will affect my kids and I don't want them to suffer by being caught out in the cross-fire between myself and their mother."

The judge replied, "I can arrest her between 9am and 3pm and have her released in time to go and pick up the kids, but it's important that we institute an arrest, so she explains in person why she keeps flouting court orders and not turning up in court. It's called a bench warrant arrest."

My fears and anxieties were somewhat allayed. I agreed to the district judge authorizing Kay's bench warrant arrest, and within two weeks, lo and behold, as the district judge had said, Kay was in court, the lioness of England had been dragged into court and actually made an appearance this time.

Kay's court appearance marked the beginning of a series of further court appearances in which the judges were trying to thrash out comprehensive child contact arrangements. There were also the financial dispute resolutions, during which I saw the seedy side of Kay's malevolent streak, as she blatantly tried to bankrupt me. In addition to arguing about paying her child maintenance, I had to pay her spousal maintenance, and she wanted a share into my lucrative teacher's salary pension. Fortunately, the judge threw this out. "Mr. Mafirakureva still has to live. Allow him to get on with his life; he has been more than reasonable to agree to take over the remaining debt from the sale of the matrimonial house. You are both young; go and start your lives afresh. I am ordering you to actively look for a job," admonished the no-nonsense judge, glaring at Kay. I think the judge had been smart enough to realize Kay had craftily ditched her job in a brazen attempt to force the courts to make me pay her spousal maintenance, but the courts were having none of Kay's antics. I think they may have been pissed off by Kay's well-documented record of previous, flagrant breaches of court orders.

The sale of the Lay Road matrimonial house was another bone of contention between Kay and me. She started chasing away real estate agents and prospective home buyers from viewing the property. It took me applying for another enforcement order again, and still Kay was not done with me. On the designated day of the exchange of contracts for the house, she blatantly refused to vacate the house, and it was only whilst I was in the midst of arranging a court-sanctioned eviction order, that one afternoon, I received a call from my estate agents dealing with the sale of the house, informing me she had finally relented and dumped the house keys at their premises the previous day. But Kay's protracted legal wrangling left me with a huge financial cost which I am happier to bear than the prospect of having continued living a lie with her in a loveless marriage which had run its course.

Over the years, I have had to deal with her vindictiveness and flare-ups of her bipolar disorder mania, manifesting itself here and there. Most prominently, though, it's been tragic how Kay has persistently failed to forge a meaningful relationship with her only daughter, Alexis. Sometimes, I have had to step in, but it is hard work dealing with Kay's obduracy and obnoxious nature. Many a time, I have inwardly remarked to myself that it must be hard the way Kays goes on about life, being perpetually angry with people and the world, particularly her own daughter, to whom Kay has now transferred the dysfunctional relationship she used to have with me. Perhaps that's the sort of life Kay enjoys, being a grumpy old git. Where she has managed to get back at me has been through her willful manipulation of the children, particularly alienating them from their father's side of the family, the Mafirakureva clan.

Kay's evisceration of the children from me was made complete by her underhanded, spiteful manipulation of both kids, which has meant they do not know or interact with any other part of my family, other than myself. As a self-styled family man, who cherishes family values, I can tell you, it hurts. Equally hurtful is the lack of a positive, meaningful relationship with both Alexis and Brooklyn, so schooled are they in mendacity that the only time they think of me is when they want money or financial favors. Goodness knows, the numerous times I've had to call them out on this, saying, "I am not a bank, Alexis. What is far more important for me is for you and I to have a proper father-daughter relationship, not these self-serving mercenary arrangements. I cannot only exist to be a birthday or Christmas presents father. Frankly, it's not on! I don't see what stops you both from having a relationship with your kith and kin, the Mafirakurevas from my side of the family, in the same way you enjoy relations with your mother's side." I doubt both children really get it, or perhaps they deliberately rebuff my entreaties for a genuine relationship not coloured by money.

In an ironic, paradoxical sense, I find resonance in words uttered by one district judge in one of our numerous court appearances with Kay: "In summing up to both of you, I have to say children deserve to have a relationship with both sides of their family, their nan, their grandpa, so they remain grounded and balanced."

"But Ms. Bvanyangu won't allow it," I replied in earnest, to which Kay aggressively butted in, "He has to pay for their air tickets to Zimbabwe if he so much wants them to visit his family, but they can only visit his family, coming from my mother's, and just so we're clear, we are only talking of day trips here."

Unperturbed, the judge went on with his words of wisdom: "Children shouldn't be caught in the middle of your differences. Children are not stupid; they are smart, and once they grow up, they may react differently to the parent they later realize was preventing contact with their other side of the family."

In many years to come, it constantly struck me poignantly how a white judge would be very much on point in encouraging and fostering family values, yet in Zimbabwe we had grown up with the impression that the white community were not so much steeped in family. How presumptuous and wrong we can be in our understanding and estimation of those from cultures different from ours. In another telling development, more an eye-opener experience to me about my white counterparts and their ways of life, I discovered one of my colleagues at Brackley, Michelle, was married to a black husband, and she would frequently extol how their children would constantly fly to Barbados during the summer holidays and at Christmas, so they spent time with their nan and gramps, as Michelle put it. "Both my husband and I are very much pro family, Kundai, and I wouldn't hear of it, denying them the chance to be with Bill's family. Even if Bill was to leave me, things would remain the way they are, the kids absolutely adore their grandparents, and no way can I deny them that."

Here was another brilliant case of a grounded, family-oriented, white woman who was very much pro-family. Again, this touched me very much, especially as it came against the backdrop in which Kay had fought tooth and nail to alienate both Alexis and Brooklyn from the Mafirakureva clan. Yet in our Shona culture, we like to pride ourselves as custodians of cultural and family values, but perhaps it's not so much a cultural thing, but more of a vindictive personality trait, with a jilted spouse, as in the case of Kay. I tried to rationalise the whole palaver.

CHAPTER 9

Little Munchkins

In all this palaver with Kay, one seemingly silent casualty stemming from our fine madness broken relationship has been the cathartic experience I have endured which looms large and is nigh conspicuous and permanently seared into my inner psyche and memory at great emotional cost. The emotional trauma of not living with my children under the same roof, witnessing them growing up, savoring every moment as they have journeyed into teenagers and subsequently young adults, has been enormous. I have this pervading deep sense of loss at not being with *"the munchkins,"* as my daughter Alexis called herself and her little brother Brooklyn in many of our outdoor jaunts, trips and excursions in the length and breadth of Buckinghamshire and Oxfordshire, during the early years when we still lived together as a family in Aylesbury. Boy, we have memories galore of us gallivanting all over in my silver Jeep Wrangler Cherokee, which my daughter absolutely adored and begged me in later years to grace her Year 11 ball with it, ostensibly to show off to her peers. "Two weeks' time is my prom daddy, can you just shoo in at my school entrance car park with your vintage Jeep Wrangler Cherokee, so my friends and other Year 11s can crane their necks out to see me waltz into it?" was a text message I received from Alexis on the occasion of her GCSE prom. This brought a smile to my face. I reflected poignantly at how she still remembered my Jeep Wrangler with fondness, even though that had been many years ago when she was an eight-year-old girl, when I used to have this car and we did our constant joyrides most weekends with her then little brother Brooklyn.

And yet Kay had had the jaw-breaking nerve, audacity, and temerity to sit before a district judge in court spouting an avalanche of lies, "Your honor, its unproductive for him to have contact and access to the children, as they don't want to see him, they don't love him. In fact, he never had any relationship with them at all when he used to live with us."

"Really Kay?"

The children, my true diamonds, of course I have missed the children terribly a lot all these years. What wouldn't I have given to have had a glamorous, affectionate relationship with both Alexis and Brooklyn, a productive relationship, which makes me to be choked up, especially when I reminisce and go down nostalgia path? The memories are wide and varied with both children, back in the early days of my marriage to their mother, before the fine madness set in. There were those myriad moments I used to take them, drive them out for what I termed, *"Daddy's day out,"* with them. We traversed the length and breadth of UK with the Jeep Wrangler, chugging along the M25 motorway, perennially on our regular trips to Legoland, for the kids thoroughly enjoyed the Legoland experience. They had requested we return on numerous occasions, "Please, Daddy, take us back to Legoland," Brooklyn had begged continuously, tugging on my arm.

"Okay, you win, young man, Legoland it will be this weekend, but there'll have to be a trade-off of some sort, if we are to shake on this deal. I will need reciprocal concessions from both you and your sister, in fact two trade-offs," I had mischievously remarked.

"Go on, I'm listening, Daddy, what's the two conditions then?" butted in Alexis, *Miss Lippy* as I had now nicknamed her on account of her being gobby and firing on all cylinders every now and then. Her limitless energy for an eight-year-old girl never ceased to amaze me. Alexis just couldn't sit still. Add to that her little brother Brooklyn whom I called *Kinetic Energy*, then the house was always a bedlam hive of activity, not that I'm complaining, it gave meaning to our then mundane lives with Kay, in the formative years, as we got to grips raising our children together.

"Homework, of course, done to high standard, and I insist you do your bedtime reading. Both those are my non-negotiable pre-conditions in exchange for a Legoland trip," I'd said, waggling my two fingers at them to drive home my point.

"But that's not fair, Daddy, Brooklyn remarked, "I do read at school, I'm not at your school, I don't need to read, I've read all the books." The poor lad carried on with his protestations, but Dad was not for turning that Tuesday evening, I remained unflinchingly firm and resolute.

"Very well then, *little munchkins,* you heard me loud and clear; either you do as you're told or there's no Legoland trip this weekend."

"All right, you win then, Daddy," the kids would grudgingly acquiesce in a chorus.

It was all done in good humour and banter of course, as I had my children's welfare at heart, particularly their educational needs. God knows, as a serving teacher myself, I didn't want them to slip behind at school, so I constantly kept them on their toes with homework checking, spellings and reading. "I am an English teacher as you both well know, and I would take it personally if you don't score high grades in English," I would often remark to them."

"Whatever, Dad!" Miss Lippy would answer back, rolling her eyes at me, but inwardly she must have been taking it in. The events of one Year 11 parents' evening vindicated her prowess and excellence in English as her teacher Ms. Pratt was gushing in her glowing eulogy of Alexis, much to my delight, "Alexis is a perfectionist in English, nigh brilliant, and if she can replicate her current performance in class in her summer exams, then I'll be seeing her in my A Level class next year in September." True to Ms. Pratt's predictions, Alexis had done brilliantly in her GCSE's, and the crowning moment for me as a dad was when she opted to study English as one of her main subjects at A Level. More to that, she smashed her GCSEs and had earned herself a place at the prestigious Royal Latin Grammar School in Buckingham.

That had been many years ago. How the wheel had turned, as I looked back at the road we've travelled with my children, even though the absent father spectre had hogged us. Still, the formative years memories of my relationship with both children, when they were young, has kept me going. Plush Wendover Woods Forestry in Tring, Buckinghamshire, was amongst some of the places of interest I used to frequent with the kids, for they so loved to grace Gruffalo the "monster." Gruffalo cut a majestic presence at Wendover Woods and was a favourite for both Alexis and Brooklyn to play and run around. "Please, Daddy, take our pictures, Alexis and me, as we're standing next to Gruffalo," Brooklyn... Brooks, as I sometimes called him, had begged in his pleading, youthful voice on one such occasion. And I was only too glad to comply, as those pictures would later be sent to me on my phone as souvenirs, and what precious memories they were, flicking through them on my phone in the serene calmness of my flat.

Watermead Park outing, a village located half a mile north of Aylesbury, was also another typical favourite outing for the children and me. On rare occasions, Kay would join us, but she would then find an excuse to want to go home early, much to the children's chagrin as they enjoyed expending their infinite energies, running around the park, and savoring the beautiful, expansive Watermead Park lake.

"Watermead is fun, Daddy," Alexis would remark excitedly.

"Why do you like it so much?"

"Aaah, I love feeding the ducks, running and chasing the little munchkin Brooklyn around the lake."

"Alexis let's play hide and seek," shouted Brooklyn, as he ran around, skipping in the grass on his little boyish feet. What a spectacle he was then in his denim blue jeans and tiny sports shoes.

There was certainly something about Watermead Park which brought to life extra vibrancy and warmth in both children. They were more alive, for want of a better phrase, if I may put it that way.

"It's raining, it's raining, Daddy, come on little munchkin, off to the car we go," Alexis had shouted as it started drizzling in Wendover Park. Meanwhile, she'd been shooting a video of our afternoon outing that day.

Ironically, I had to use some of these myriad pictures and video footage taken by Alexis in court to push back Kay's puerile lies that I never had a relationship with the children and that was why I shouldn't be allowed to see them, and they didn't want to see me anyway. How can we be so depraved as adults if it comes to this? It didn't sound right to me that I had to be made to prove the obvious, that like any normal loving parent, I had had a loving relationship with my own children, notwithstanding the divorce. Relationships fail, but people can remain on amicable terms, especially where there were minor kids, as in my case with Kay.

Waddesdon Manor country house grounds in Waddesdon village, just outside Aylesbury, was another one of our frequented places with the children, where we savored its architecture and were taken in by the historical significance of the place. Then, there was Gulliver's World theme park resort in Milton Keynes, where Brooklyn would squeal in unmitigated delight, firmly ensconced in the sky-high rides, as he in his childish innocence, called me a "wimp" when I playfully looked terrified and scared to go on these swings and train rollercoaster rides, which was hilarious to the little boy.

"Oh, don't be such a wimp, Daddy, go on! Let's go again on the crazy train rollercoaster ride, please, Daddy," Brooklyn would earnestly beg as I feigned my horror on going back on those gut-wrenching train rides, much to his delight and continued insistence, as he yelled in excitement at my palpable "fear" of rollercoasters.

Woburn Safari park visits in Woburn, Bedfordshire also had searing memories for us especially that fateful Saturday morning when a cheetah had had the cheek to settle on the bonnet of our car and that quietened the mighty voluble Brooklyn much to Alexis's delight. "Aah, have you seen the mighty Brooklyn is quite Daddy?"

"Shut up, will you Alexis," Brooklyn had quietly hissed back to Alexis, as his eyes remained transfixed on the errant cheetah on our car bonnet.

So, I did have a positive relationship with my kids early on in the marriage at some point, before this fine madness set in, and don't let anyone tell you otherwise. I won't hear of it. Where my children are concerned, I've always striven to be involved in their lives and stepped in promptly, barring *those lost years* when contact was hampered and perennially obstructed against my will. Let those falsehoods remain, as they're porkies, fibs peddled against me by Kay to bolster her facile narrative that I was some kind of nefarious Count Dracula monster in relation to my children. Far from it, nothing could be further from the truth, for want of a cliché. Did we have to go down this route? Kay knew very well in her heart of hearts, in her very bosom, that I adored my children as they meant a lot to me and they will always be *my true munchkins*. I don't need to prove to anyone that I had a viable relationship with my kids, in any case, my conscience is my master.

CHAPTER 10

The Brackley Days - Reflections of an Invisible Man

I cut my professional teeth into English schools at The Brackley School in Brackley, Oxfordshire, then called Brackley Community College (BCC), in September 2002. I arrived at BCC, a fresh-faced youth, bristling with limitless energy and exuberance, having taught English successfully in Zimbabwe for over seven years. There was a springy step in my gait, quite a swagger of confidence, reminiscent of Andy Dufresne's swagger of self-worth and confidence in *The Shawshank Redemption film*. I was raring to go in my first teaching post in England. I had attended my interview in June 2002, taking a day's break from my valeting job in Aylesbury, after getting much grief from my two Ghanaian co-valets, Mike and Albert.

The interview was friendly and overseen by then Head of English at the school, Roland Kinnock who, unbeknown to me at the time, was to become a close, loyal, and genuine friend over many years to come. Roland took me on a tour of the school early in the morning, prior to my interview, which was slated for later that afternoon with the affable Ms. Cynthia Grayling, the head teacher. Also attending the interviews that day was Clare Morgan, who incidentally got the job as another co-English teacher, and we became long-serving colleagues in the Brackley English Department.

In looking back, I have a plethora of fond memories in relation to my days at Brackley, a place where I spent over two decades of my professional life. That's quite a feat, something I hadn't achieved even in my native Zimbabwe. My remit at Brackley was Teacher of English, with special responsibility for Media Studies. The media bit is quite interesting for me. Growing up as a little boy in Dangamvura, Mutare, I had always harboured ambitions to be a journalist. No wonder I was something of a local celebrity in my teen days; I used to prodigiously write letters to the editor of our local newspaper in Mutare, *The Manica Post*, highlighting pertinent issues in our community. Once I wrote a letter about police brutality and football players changing their uniforms in public, also urinating publicly, as there were no dressing rooms at Dangamvura football grounds at the local Beit Hall.

Then there were also those days of youthful exuberance when I had flirted with writing in high school, immoderately churning out short stories and poetry, which I read and performed as part of the Manicaland Writers Association (MWA) cohort at Mutare Museum. I look back at those days with nostalgic fondness, as my childhood friend Peter Chemvura and I, likeminded "sods," mingled and rubbed shoulders with other greats, such as the late Geoffrey Kuhudzai, my dear friend Anthony Marembo (RIP to both), Barbra Faindi, Ethel Kabwato, and Pathisa Nyathi, among other luminaries. Geoffrey Kuhudzai left a lasting impression on me, courtesy of his charismatic oratory. Incidentally, in later years, teaching in Honde Valley, at Gatsi Secondary School, I was to become close buddies with his adopted son Patrick, who remains a friend to this day.

I would later revisit police brutality in my writing at University, maligning the heavy-handed nature of police response, particularly their brute force against students' demonstrations. Fiery and militant those days as an undergraduate, I used to sport a white brotherhood tee shirt emblazoned with the words, *"Say NO to police brutality; UZ students' union in defiance of maladministration and police brutality!"* On the front of the tee shirt was also written another message of bravado directed to the riot police: *"An injury to one is an injury to all."* The brotherhood tee shirt was later to be a key talking point between my brother Kian and me, with Kian always reminiscing how he adored it. It later became part of his teenage fashion that he used to woo girlfriends. Through contributions to local media houses in Harare, and participating at the famed Zimbabwe International Book Fair, I stood on rooftops calling out all forms of social injustice and excesses of the post-independence government, the sum of which resulted in me spending some nights as a guest of the state at Avondale Police Station. Still, it kept the writing spirit in me fired up, notwithstanding the incarceration woes.

"Why don't you tone down a bit, Kundai, we don't want to lose you," Mother would earnestly admonish me each time I had brushes with law enforcement agents and state security operatives over my dabbling in student politics at university and inviting the ire of university authorities, the brutal Mugabe regime, and its sadistic riot police hoodlums.

"But someone has to make a principled stand, Mum," I would shoot back at her in all politeness.

"Your problem, Kundai, is that you're too headstrong for your own good. Just like your father, no one can tell you otherwise, once you have an idea in that big head of yours. An apple doesn't fall far from the tree. At least I've tried to make you see some sense. My conscience is clean as your mother," she remarked, wringing her hands in frustration.

Much as I commiserated with Mother, I was not for turning. I understood earlier on in these formative stages that such was the role of the writer, to be the soul and conscience of the nation, and if reprisals arose, then let it be it's a clear case of occupational hazards. I vividly recall in the university student body we used to eulogize ourselves with the accolade, "Voice of the voiceless," as we were wont to champion social justice issues and stood up for the marginalized and downtrodden populace then.

By the time I enrolled at the University of Zimbabwe in the early 1990s, they did not offer a Journalism degree, so I studied English instead. In my mind, it made logical sense to study English, as I rationalised within myself, English and Journalism were closely related, and perhaps I was right, as one needs English as a medium of communication, especially when working for world media houses. I guess writing was always part of me; at UZ, I dallied with writing under the auspices of Budding Writers Association of Zimbabwe, (BWAZ) with my contemporary, Sigauke and his mate, then popular news anchor Alson Mufiri. Upon graduating from the University of Zimbabwe, I enrolled for a BA in Media Studies degree with the Zimbabwe Open University (ZOU). We were the pioneers on this programme, with some other colleagues like Maboreke, Kwari, and Madera, among others. I appear to be digressing, but the media bit is important, for I got my teaching job at Brackley purely on the strength of my postgraduate studies in Media. I had successfully completed two years of the four-year programme with ZOU.

My memories of Brackley are wide and varied. The first few years were hectic and eventful, as I strove to settle and acclimatise to a new environment and new culture altogether. Teaching English kids was a nigh difficult experience for one used to compliant Zimbabwean kids. The first shock for me was when I walked into the classroom, one Tuesday morning in September 2002, and the kids kept on talking over me, even when I asked them to be quiet. "Good morning, and please be quiet," I entreated, to which they mimicked, "Good morning and please be quiet, Sir." This was to be the beginning of learning the skills associated with that two-letter phrase I came to hate so much: *classroom management.* I quickly learned how to jump through the hoops so I would be able to have the kids on my side and thus be able to teach them. The teaching days tended to fluctuate; some days were rowdy, and some were fairly okay. The saving grace for me was that I taught sixth form students and that's where I was able to effectively establish myself well as a consummate professional.

The first time I set my eyes on my sixth form students at Brackley, I couldn't believe they were actually students; they looked bigger in stature than me. *Would they listen to me in the classroom?* was one of the thoughts and fears which nibbled and tugged at my heart, but I need not have had any qualms. Sixth form teaching was to constitute the forte of my teaching career, not only at Brackley but at other schools where I taught within England, as my rapport with sixth form students was always top notch.

Within my first year at Brackley, the maiden exam results for Media were like an ego-boosting endorsement for me; all my twenty A-Level Media class students fared very well, attaining at least a grade C or better. That was huge for me, that moment. A couple of names stick out, but I will mention Eleanor Wilson and Rebecca Danbury, those two brightest minds, my first A's in A-Level Media in England. Both girls were to later distinguish themselves in their later lives, Eleanor becoming a high-level editor-in-chief for *Elsevier Magazine* and also working for *The Guardian* newspaper in a high-ranking role. Eleanor successfully carved out a flamboyant media career for herself. Unbeknown to me at the time, the success of my maiden A-Level Media group was to mark the commencement of a glittering career for me, in which I carved an indelible mark into the Brackley Media Department folklore history. Successive media groups were to excel consistently, year-in and year-out, and the Media Department grew in leaps and bounds. Such was my success that in a 2012 Ofsted report, a dark year for the school in which it was put in special measures, the report singled out Media Studies amongst a few other courses in which the attainment results were consistently higher over many years. Such endorsement, to "the black man," as I inwardly called myself, was welcome.

In Zimbabwe, I had obtained a bachelor's degree in English, which was considered a teaching degree. Thus, I had gone straight into teaching after graduating from university. However, I did not have a formal teaching qualification, and at Brackley, the affable Cynthia called me to her office one morning and said, "Good morning, Kundai. I just wanted to check with you. How are you doing? Settling down?"

"All right, Ms. Grayling, thank you."

She replied, "No need to call me Ms., I understand it's difficult for you, this first name basis thing, but Cynthia will do."

She was right, the first few days, I struggled in calling adults like my Head of School by their first names. I remember constantly calling the head of Sixth Form, Mr. Williams and he would relentlessly correct me, with, "Just Ken is all right, Kundai." It takes time adjusting to some of these cultural norms. Inwardly, I always felt like it was disrespectful calling people by their first names, especially when they were older than you, as was the case with Cynthia.

"We are pleased with your progress here at Brackley, Kundai. We have decided to put you on a Graduate Teacher Programme, (GTP)," Cynthia went on, her eyes peering at me over her glasses, with her sweet smile, as ever.

"Ah, thank you, Ms. Grayling...sorry, I meant Cynthia," I replied stunned, with this beautiful gem of news coming from her.

"Trevor Phillips, the staff development manager, will be in touch to oversee your training. It's an on-the-job teacher training programme," Cynthia added, "and so you won't lose your job. You will still carry on with your full teaching load, though at times you will need to go to Oxford University for research seminars and classes, to mingle and network with other interns."

I finally managed to compose myself and thanked Cynthia heartily for this arrangement, which was to consolidate my professional standing as a teacher in England.

And so, it happened, in 2003 I commenced my on-the-job

teacher training, called GTP at Brackley Community College. True to Cynthia's word, Trevor, the staff development manager, another lovely chappie, organised and facilitated my training. Three others overseas-trained teachers like me were also on the programme. These were Lamine, Lynley, and Melthem. It was difficult striking a balance between a full-time teaching job and teacher training, maintaining a portfolio of qualified teacher status standards (QTS) evidence, having to contend with lesson observations from my head of department, and external tutors from Oxford University. To that, add on the demands of a young family to contend with. Still, I looked forward to those Wednesdays, when we had to leave school early to go into Oxford for our pedagogy training sessions. I made some good friendships there: Eva from The Cherwell School and Iden from The Marlborough School.

The year 2004 saw me successfully completing my teacher training, though my day of assessment was not without drama and incidents. I arrived at school early in the morning, armed with my voluminous lever arch file containing all my QTS teacher standards evidence. Regarding anything to do with organizing paperwork, and putting it together in a file, I knew I was a master. It was my forte. I was and am a stickler for paperwork. Perhaps where I was not so confident in the assessment process was that the assessor would have to observe me teach an hour's lesson across two key stages; in my case, my assessor Janet, a bespectacled, plump, middle-aged woman, came to watch me first with a Year 7 English group, and later after break, a Year 10 English group. I felt the Year 7 English lesson didn't go well because I had planned a role play activity. Whilst working in small groups of 3s and 4s, a group of girls decided to ruin it for me by continuously giggling when it was time for their group delivery. The Year 10 lesson made me feel confident; the majority of students were mostly engaged with their work.

Janet, the Teacher Training Agency (TTA) assessor, was very generous and complimentary to me in her debrief at the end of the assessment day. "Well, Kundai, congratulations on becoming a fully-fledged English Teacher," she said, stretching her hand out to shake mine, as I sat down in the English office.

"Thank you, Janet," I returned her hand gesture as I sat down.

"Well, how do you feel about the day?" she enquired, looking at me intently.

I thought perhaps this was a trick question, so I politely looked for a modest response. "Ah, okay, I would say, apart from those giggling girls in Year 7," I remarked.

"Well, if anything, Kundai, the good thing is, you challenged them for their silly behaviour," Janet said, adding, "I would never fail anyone for silly behaviour, unless you hadn't challenged it, then I would certainly pull you up on that one."

"The other thing is," Janet carried on, "Your QTS portfolio is one of the best I have assessed in many years, Kundai! Congratulations again. How did you do it?" She added, "And I also thoroughly enjoyed your diary, or reflective commentary, over the course of your training, especially the bits about you being petulant to your daughter as you were putting together the portfolio."

"Oh, poor old Alexis, my little one," I chuckled.

"Anyway, you've done very well, Kundai. Accept my congratulations once more." As she spoke, both the Head of English, Roland and his Deputy, Helen, came into the English office, and they both congratulated me, as well.

"Here is what will happen," Janet went on, "I will communicate my decision to the Teacher Training Agency (TTA) England, who will then liaise with the General Teaching Council for England, (GTC), and so Kundai should receive his GTC Teacher Reference number and certificate, thereafter. Once more, my warm congratulations to you, Roland and Helen, for mentoring Kundai. You have a great asset there," she said, nodding towards me. "Look after him." Both Roland and Helen thanked Janet as they accompanied her out, leaving me in a euphoric state.

My happiness, however, was short-lived, for the man I had come to rely on as a mentor, friend, and guiding light, Roland, quit his headship of the English department shortly after, opting instead to go and work as a consultant at Oxfordshire County Council. "Good people don't stay in a place for long," I said to Roland after he informed me of his imminent departure. "The good ones, like you, mate, go on to spread their goodness and kind nature to other parts of the world where they are needed," I went on to say.

That night, in the privacy of my bedroom, I silently sobbed, mourning the leaving of Roland, a man whom I had come to regard as a pillar of strength and support during my formative years at Brackley. Call it a sense of déjà vu, but somehow, with Roland gone, I felt exposed and vulnerable, and it wasn't long before my fears were vindicated. In no time, I fell out spectacularly with the new Head of English, Helen, who took over Roland's position.

For someone who had received a glowing eulogy on my teaching prowess from Janet the external assessor, suddenly, according to Helen, I couldn't get it right anymore. That dreaded term, *classroom management*, came to haunt me. "You have no classroom management skills," Helen would harangue me. "The kids are not learning anything from you, I'm afraid. I'm on the side of the kids," she railed on, and further pontificated, "Whatever decision I make, it's for the good of the kids and the school."

Then one day, she came and started asking me about the precise nature and details of my contract. Looking back, my naiveté at the time seriously let me down at this point. For had that been happening now, I do not see how my head of department had anything to do with my employment contract, as it would look sinister to me, conflating my so-called lack of classroom management skills with wanting to know the tenure of my employment. *Hmmm, something fishy was brewing here,* I couldn't avoid deducing. It didn't take long for my suspicions to be confirmed. Within a week or so, Helen came to deliver the Sword of Damocles to me herself, after sitting me down in the English office. The irony had probably been lost on her, since it was the exact venue where Janet, the teacher training assessor, had eulogized me previously, effectively saying to them, "Look after this young man, he is an asset."

After an awkward silence, Helen cleared her throat. "Well, I don't know how to say this, Kundai, but it appears you are mistaken that you are on a continuous permanent contract. I have checked with HR and you're on a fixed contract, which finishes with the end of this academic year, summer 2005." She went on like an automaton, "So, for your own good and professional growth, it may be wise for you to look elsewhere." I was dumbstruck with this bombshell from Helen. Noticing my numbness, she tried to soften the blows. "We have two English positions, and you are free to apply against Cheryl and Rose, the two other current interns in the department. But you have to know, they've been brilliant, here. The kids like them. I really think, for your own good, it's better to leave this place now; you've done your training. Go elsewhere, adopt a new persona, and forge a new identity." That was Helen to me, twisting the knife further in my back.

I am normally astute at reading people, and although I could see through Helen's animosity towards me, I somehow subjected myself to the indignity of putting in an application for a job I had been brazenly told was not mine. It was a no-brainer. After going through the façade of the job interview, I didn't get it; Cheryl and Rose, the anointed ones, were appointed, two blonde girls in an exclusively white, middle class Brackley area. It was all set for the English Department. It's only now, when I look back, with the hindsight of the Black Lives Matter Movement, that I see the subtle nature of some of my experiences at English schools.

Following my failure to land the English teaching job, I approached the head teacher, Cynthia Grayling, and requested a change of mentor. I had commenced my mandatory one-year induction and I did not feel Helen would be a neutral and objective mentor to me anymore, following her bias against me. Cynthia was astute and must have empathized with my aggrieved nature, so she acquiesced to my request and Jo Waverly became my mentor. Jo, that bastion of kindness and compassion, was to become another good friend of mine over many years, like Roland. Jo was able to successfully sign me off for the one-term induction period I completed at Brackley. The erudite and kind-hearted Jo was to equally help me with job applications and interview role-playing rehearsals.

As luck would have it, in June 2005, I went back to Princes Risborough School, (PRS), my home for six weeks in 2003, when I had been there doing my mandatory six weeks placement. As it turned out, two candidates had been shortlisted for the English teacher jobs, myself and the inimitable Zettie Jones, who was to later have such a reverberating influence in my life. We were both delighted to see each other, and as we spoke prior to the interview, we both wished each other well. If we didn't get the job, we promised to keep in touch as friends. Of course, that was before Rowan Sharper called us both into his office after the interviews had been done.

In talking to Zettie later as she drove me home to Aylesbury, we remarked how strange it was for Rowan to have summoned us two candidates together for an interview debrief. But of course, Rowan's calling us together soon became clear to us. "Zettie and Kundai, I am delighted to appoint you both as English teachers at Princes Risborough School," Rowan boomed at us, smiling and extending his hands to a bemused Zettie and me.

It took a bit of time for us to compose ourselves, and Zettie fired back, "Thank you, Rowan, but we were under the impression you only wanted one English teacher, according to the job advert."

"On point, Zet, on point," Rowan remarked, grinning widely at us. "We certainly wanted to recruit one candidate for the post, but we have been highly impressed by the high calibre of both candidates. So, I have decided to appoint you two," he said again, smiling and turning to the other interview panelist. "Ms. Kent, here, she shares similar sentiments with me about you two," he chuckled, as Ms. Kent, Head of School Governors, nodded in acquiescence.

Zettie and I were visibly overwhelmed at this bit of staggering good news, and so we talked about nothing else in Zettie's Ford Fiesta as she drove me home that nice, sunny afternoon. "Perhaps we were meant to be together, Kuu," Zettie was wont to later remind me, many a time. "Look at it, Kuu, I don't believe in coincidence for no reason, but look at it, we were both appointed for the same job, at a time they'd only advertised for one post! If this is not a signal to you about us, then I don't know what is." Maybe, she was right.

Traditionally the academic term for schools in England starts in September, but Rowan made it clear he wanted Zettie and me to commence duty on June 1, as opposed to the September start. This arrangement suited Zet well; she'd recently graduated from uni, so a June start meant she would be paid over the summer holiday. For me, I had to negotiate with my head teacher Cynthia to release me early from my contract. Good old Cynthia readily agreed to release me, and so with a heavy heart, I bid farewell to Brackley Community College on 31st May 2005 for a new chapter in my life.

CHAPTER 11

PRS Interlude

I aptly call my stint at Princes Risborough School (PRS) an interlude, as I only spent two years there. By January 1, 2008, I was back at Brackley again, much to my delight. Life at PRS was equally eventful, albeit my being there so briefly. It was made more exciting by my intimate, passionate relationship with Zet. At first, it was surreal, working together in the same department with Zet, and knowing I would be banging her in the evening. Zet didn't make things any easier for me; she was very tactile in public and an exhibitionist in her affections towards me in public. A random kiss, hair stroking, a gentle grab from behind, or cuddling, she simply couldn't keep her hands off me. Once I tried to chide her, to no avail,

"Why do you like this PDA business Zet? It makes me uneasy," I said. She laughed me off, "Unease, mister prim and proper, huh...Well, better get used to it, honey, for I like to publicly stake out my territory, so other vultures keep away."

That was Zet for you. What I never could understand was how she reconciled my double dipping, as in our relationship whilst on paper I still remained married to Kay. Zet was a very good listener each time, I poured out my heart to her about Kay's antics. She never uttered a word of criticism against Kay. *What is your game plan, Zet?* I kept asking myself. Whatever game she played, she warmed herself to my heart. We had a profound connection, Zet and I, a connection which, at times, was telepathic. One thing about Zet, she was genuine. She loved me for me.

More so, with both our after-sex heart to heart pillow confessions in which we pledged to be true to each other.

I quickly settled down to the mundane PRS life, which had its own challenges and idiosyncrasies. The English department colleagues were lovely, nice people, led by Mike Jones, a father figure to me (no relation to Zet). Then there were Sally and Dawn, my two esteemed mentors, as I was due to do two more terms in to complete my teacher training induction. Unlike Brackley, where induction was a two-way thing between the teacher and his/her mentor, PRS ran a different system, whereby staff induction for newly qualified teachers (NQTs) like me was overseen by the school's staff development manager, one Jacky Pinhead. She was a power-crazed megalomaniac, who would have turned Napoleon Bonaparte pale in insignificance with her zealotry. I don't know whether it was in her mind only, but Jacky deified herself as a demigod, and glorified herself as having dungeons where she could dump naughty kids. I am not even sure whether this was meant to be funny and scare children or staff, but I took it in bad taste. I did not support that someone could eulogize workplace bullying as worthy of being a trite laughing matter.

In hindsight, Jacky was a twisted, sexist, sadist, who enjoyed terrorising male teachers. It was all about power, her aphrodisiac. In retrospect, that was workplace bullying left unchecked. It is wrong to condone such awful workplace practices as what transpired at PRS. "Rowan the headteacher is a clever bastard who uses Jacky to do his dirty bidding at PRS," as Dennis, one of my astute colleagues, remarked.

Two terms elapsed under Jacky's hard regime and I successfully completed my induction and became a fully qualified teacher and thus acquired my (QTS) in England, but that had come at the heavy toll of being obsequious and servile to Jacky's every whim and fancy.

I am not stupid.

One survival trick I learnt with white people in England was to play the politics of survival; sometimes you had to act the fool and know when to say something or keep your mouth shut. I had learnt that from some of my black colleagues who were radical and fiery, along with knowing how they had been summarily dismissed upon flimsy grounds at the behest of Jacky. There was always the omnipresent threat of constructive dismissal hanging over our heads, like the proverbial Sword of Damocles.

Once, a Zambian friend of mine called Tom, who was a brilliant science teacher, got a negative observation report from Jacky. Cheeky Tom requested of Jacky, "Ms. Pinhead, I would like to come and observe one of your lessons so that I can learn some good classroom practices," to which Jacky acquiesced. For one with such an inflated ego and misplaced sense of importance, it was bound to be in the affirmative.

And so, the story goes, one afternoon, Tom sat at the back of Jacky's classroom making detailed notes as Jacky was foaming and frothing at the mouth, issuing threats and intimidating students under the guise of teaching. By the end of her lesson, Tom calmly sat down with Jacky for a debrief. "Well, Jacky, I'm afraid you don't practice what you preach," Tom remarked calmly. He continued, "To begin with, you didn't write today's date on the board. The kids were continuously talking out of turn over you, in spite of your threats..." Tom told us Jacky never allowed him to finish his debrief. She stormed out of the classroom, stony faced, straight to her puppet master Rowan, and within a fortnight, Tom was no longer at PRS. We all commiserated with Tom, as he was a family man with a family to look after, but the majority of staff gave him kudos for dressing down Jacky the bully. We constantly eulogized Tom amid chuckles in the staffroom.

On completion of my induction, I was due to go up the upper pay scale from Main Pay Scale 6 to Upper Pay Scale 1 (UPS1). Usually, the way it worked was, a teacher would put together a portfolio of evidence demonstrating how they met the upper threshold pay standards. The portfolio would then be assessed by the head teacher, who would make the salary increment recommendation to the board of governors, who in turn would subsequently ratify this. To my white colleagues, crossing the threshold was a mere formality; I doubt they even had to go through the onerous process of putting together a portfolio of evidence. My skepticism on how the upper pay scale application process was heavily skewed and tilted against ethnic minorities like me was confirmed when one of my white colleagues at PRS, Gareth, nonchalantly mentioned in the staffroom, amongst other staff members, how Rowan had asked him to submit a short email requesting UPS1 progression. That was it! He was promptly moved up the pay grade, just like that! I submitted the voluminous lever arch file I had meticulously put together over several weeks with a fine-tooth comb trawl of supporting documents, and my application was promptly rejected by Rowan. In his words, I had just completed teacher training and how dare I aspire for something beyond me. "The upper pay scale is for experienced practitioners who have proved themselves," I was firmly told, but perhaps Rowan hadn't realised I knew my rights, having done thorough background research. I knew I was standing on solid ground.

Jacky was roped in to whip me into line. She reiterated Rowan's patronising remarks and gave a condescending little speech, "You don't deserve the upper pay scale because you've just finished your induction. You don't have much teaching experience. In any case, it's meant for well-experienced teachers."

"Well, I respectfully disagree, Ms. Pinhead," I remarked to her, "And I will be consulting my professional association for the way forward." To which Jacky replied, "Of course, it's well within your rights to do so." There was something ominous about the way Jacky said her last words. I am usually good at reading people's body language, and something told me that by deciding to square up with both Jacky and Rowan, I had crossed the proverbial red line.

I turned to Lucia, an Italian colleague who was the NASWUT school rep, and incidentally on very good terms with Rowan, whom she referred to as a friend. I explained to Lucia how at my last school, Cynthia, the head teacher, had taken into account my seven years teaching experience in Zimbabwe by putting me on Main Pay Scale 4, which acknowledgment Cynthia stated in her letter. Lovely woman Cynthia was.

Lucia was visibly pleased to see Cynthia's letter, which corroborated my explanations, and she did assure me, "Yes, we do have a credible case, Kundai. We are good to go!"

And so, it happened. I waited for several weeks to let this whole thing die down, then I proceeded to book for an appointment with Rowan. I played my cards close to my chest on the day of the meeting. As we walked into Rowan's office together with Lucia, he asked, surprised to see her, "Why is she here?" I remarked, "For moral support." Surprisingly, Rowan was okay with our meeting, and surprise, surprise, he agreed to look into my UPS1 application, (which he had previously declined). So, I left my folder with him, and it was he and Lucia having their "friendly" chat as I vacated his office. A few weeks later, I got an official letter from Rowan in my pigeonhole, confirming my pay award had been successful and I had been moved to Upper Pay Scale 1.

It was a pyrrhic victory for me; my ordeal with Jacky was about to commence. As I had cleverly sussed out, Jacky never forgave me for daring to stand up for my rights and asking to be considered for the threshold salary increment. Within days of receiving the confirmation of my pay increase, my ordeal started. Jacky started hounding me in my lessons. She could be lurking in the corridors or she could just turn up, unannounced. Then the "classroom management" buzzword restarted with her.

CHAPTER 12

Exit Interviews Façade

In a clear case of nihilistic cynicism, at times, this wanton display of workplace bullying, systematic intimidation, and harassment against staff was selectively applied to other white colleagues to give it a veneer of legitimacy and impartiality that not only one ethnic group was being targeted. And this so happened to Sue Harper, one of my esteemed colleagues at PRS. A brilliant Sixth Form Biology teacher with a background in further education, she became easy fodder for Jacky, ostensibly because of her supposedly poor classroom management skills with the junior classes. And when she took some time off due to illness, Jacky struck.

Ultimately, we were persistently bullied and eventually hounded out of the school by Jacky, but the establishment had the nerve to conduct what they termed exit interviews, "So we can be able to see what we are doing well and where we need to improve, moving forward." Seriously, one couldn't make up this self-serving narcissistic stuff! You hound people out of their jobs, and yet you still want to hear what they think of you, and your policies. That was Princes Risborough's praxis. Princes Risborough is a township around nine miles from Aylesbury, where I had lived with Kay and our children.

In Sue, they had a different character. Recounting back to Zet and me, Sue said there was no holding back; she gave it to them, no holds barred, in a jaw-dropping exit interview. "Well, I just had to be honest, didn't I?" remarked the affable Sue amid intermittent laughter and chuckles. "I told Rowan and his 'mistress' Jacky that there are ways to get the best out of adults other than bullying."

I could pretty much relate with Sue's torment at the hands of the insidious duo, Jacky and Rowan, as it reminded me of a similar experience when, one morning, I had unexpected car problems. Once my car broke down on my way to school, God forbid! I promptly informed the school of my mishap and how I was waiting to be towed away by my breakdown cover recovery vehicle. The breakdown cover recovery car took a long time to arrive and, in the end, I couldn't make it to school that day. Being the consummate professional that I am, however, I kept the school informed of my predicament as it unfolded. You can imagine my utmost shock the next morning, first thing, I arrived at school to a blistering, long email tirade in my inbox from Rowan the Head. He banged on and on about my responsibility to always put the kids first. "You should have left your car by the road and proceeded to school. We are a school well served by public transport, both rail and road, or better still, get a taxi," jumped out snippets from Rowan's snorty email. That was the nature of the man, so petty and trite, always majoring in minors and hopelessly wanting on depth and substance. I let it pass. We live to fight another day.

In scenes reminiscent of Ralph Ellison's *Invisible Man*'s nameless narrator, Rowan was to exact his revenge on me, reprising the *"keep the nigger-boy running"* theme by blocking my UPS2 salary progression when I returned to Brackley school.

I can't say that I hadn't seen it coming. Rowan's language in his exit interview with me had been ominous. "You let us down after investing in you, giving you your threshold, and now you're going back to your former school. You've made your decision, haven't you? There's nothing we can do about it," he said with an air of feigned resignation.

Two years later, now back at Brackley, and Cynthia needed a

reference recommendation from my former school, PRS. Rowan and Jacky had a field day as they feasted on my carcass. They wrote me a damning reference in which they alleged, left, right and centre, that I was an inept classroom teacher. The silver lining to this whole charade was that I had handwritten lesson observation reports from both Rowan and Jacky which attested to my brilliance as a classroom practitioner! This helped me expose their hypocrisy and double standards. To further give credence to their misrepresentation of my classroom practice, they further alleged, so bad was my teaching, that they'd had to hire a coach from the county to tutor me. Of course, nothing could have been farther from the truth than these aspersions they cast on my persona. Far from it, a county coach was part of Bucks County Council's induction program, which was standard practice enjoyed by all newly qualified teachers undergoing their induction. In my heart, I was vindicated that I had made the right move exiting PRS, even though it meant leaving Zet behind.

Half the time at PRS, staff were routinely subjected to threats by Rowan, such as, "I will charge you for misconduct if you are off school for no reason. I'll make sure I dock your salary." And it so happened, my other colleague, Belinda, fell into the latter category when she had to take legitimate time off school after her daughter Milly nearly lost her life in an electrocution accident at home. Such was the lack of compassion with the monster that PRS was. Belinda nearly loses her child in a tragic domestic accident, and her salary is docked for missing a day or two of school for such an unquestionably humane, legitimate reason. I and many other colleagues were appalled by this crassness and wanton cruelty. The PRS juggernaut was like a monstrous vampire, out to crush staff whom it was meant to protect. It took a letter from Belinda's solicitors for Rowan to rescind his decision to dock the former's salary.

Those more perceptive, like me, Zet, and other members of staff, were able to see through the vacuous facade of Rowan,

Jacky and their other senior management underlings. I remember Denis remarking, "People like Jacky and Lorraine, they're shit, and they know it. That's why they've been here for so many years. Beyond Princes Risborough, they're nonentities, they wouldn't make it out there." I must admit, I entirely agreed with Denis' sentiments.

True to our prognosis of these charlatans, a few years down the line, PRS went into special measures. Jacky was one of the first members of staff to throw in the towel and opt for early retirement, rather than be subjected to the very scrutiny which had been the hallmark of her professional life. Rowan was unceremoniously given his marching orders after persistent poor Ofsted ratings for the school. I'm told his last days were spent in an anonymous alcoholic-rehabilitation home. Talk of chickens coming home to roost, Rowan would be heard ranting and raving to those who cared to listen about how brilliant he'd been as a head teacher, only to be misunderstood by his ungrateful staff and community.

And then, bizarrely, I started having that recurrent dream, years later after I had left PRS. I'm not sure whether it was something playing on my subconscious. For they say dreams are the substance of our thoughts, don't they? There was many a time when I woke up, sweating profusely and with disturbing heart palpitations, and in all the cases, it was because of the recurrent dream I had had, having gone back to PRS as a member of their teaching staff again. I always woke up chiding myself on my poor insight and lack of judgement on why I would ever contemplate going back to that place or blaming myself relentlessly for why I had gone back, given my traumatic experiences and interactions there. Of course, the relief was always uplifting upon waking up, and realising it was only but a dream. Perhaps PRS scarred and traumatised me; certainly, PRS haunted my dreams.

Key lessons I learnt from PRS, though, were the lengths I had to go to fight for myself, for seemingly ordinary things like a salary increment that I was meant to have. I am glad I can't say I was being paranoid, because even Zet, my lover, did concur with me in calling out, what she termed white privilege at the time. White privilege! I was later to encounter this term many times in my professional career and spheres of personal life. I liked Zet for her honesty and clarity of thought, even though we were two people from across two diametrically opposed divides. Zet was always objective in articulating some of the subtle "unfair" treatment I experienced at the hands of my white colleagues: the needless nit picking of irrelevant stuff, like the dreaded classroom management moniker; the patronising hand-holding stuff; and the disproportionate lesson drop-ins or "unannounced learning walks," as they tried to sugar coat them.

The day after I got an email from Jacky requesting to have a meeting with me in relation to my classroom management skills, I got an invitation for a Head of Media Studies job at my previous school, Brackley Community College. Talk of excellent timing, for me that is.

CHAPTER 13

Brackley – The Second Coming

Introspection

In my early years settling down at Brackley School, amongst some of the challenges I faced were some parents insisting their children be taught by a different teacher, once they realised, I was black and spoke with an accent. It was a particularly big deal to a section of these parents who couldn't fathom a non-white teaching their children English. Sometimes, their sentiments were communicated to me directly at parents' evenings by some of the less tactful parents, or I could pick it up from the kids themselves. This is where Roland, my then head of English, was brilliant; he knew how to effectively manage such parents. In one phone conversation to a parent, he told them to count their blessings, because their child was lucky to have Mr. Mafirakureva. "He is an extremely qualified English teacher, and if you are unhappy with him, then you are welcome to look elsewhere to place your child." Good old Roland, you could count on him to stand by you as a fellow colleague. The same was true of Roland's modus operandi in confronting kids who demonstrated racist attitudes towards me by way of imitating my accent, or some would whine, "I can't understand him; I prefer Miss."

I don't know whether I was initially naïve, I chose not to see it, or perhaps my awareness grew as the scales increasingly fell from my eyes. Yet I found myself having to increasingly prove to my new colleagues that I was worthy to be called an English teacher, particularly to the new head of English, Elaine Finicky. I worked with her on my second coming. It was clearly palpable from the onset, Elaine didn't think English could be taught by a black person, let alone someone like me with a heavy Zimbabwean accent. Once she corrected me on what dramatic irony was and was not, after I alluded to what I termed "ironic situations" in Alanis Morissette's *Ironic* song. That's how pedantic and trite Elaine was. Sadly, I had a fractious relationship with her for the three years she was Head of English at Brackley.

She was exceedingly pedantic and believed in needless micromanagement, where she would patronise and subject me to her humiliating, microscopic gaze of my practice, as if I were a novice in teaching. Once I snapped angrily at her, "Look Elaine, with all due respect to you, I am not a novice in teaching, and I don't need to be chaperoned." At times she would pull me up with her acquiescing sidekick, the second in English, Alison Prior, over trivial things like: "Your marking and feedback to students is not thorough enough." Once, they both subjected me to an intensive grilling on why my books hadn't been marked for some time; and yet they were both aware I was trying to deal with a recent, tragic family bereavement of someone close. I was horrified and appalled by their callousness.

Increasingly, my professional relationship with then Head of English Finicky turned perennially difficult with her micromanagement style scaling greater heights, by the day. As she ratcheted up her war of attrition against me, I started keeping a diary of events in which I detailed her emotional abuse of me. This relentless harangue encompassed the avalanche of emails from her, with unrealistic demands and delivery time frames, which constantly clogged my school email inbox first thing each morning, throughout the teaching day, and even sometimes late at night after school. I swear Finicky had no life at all to talk of. I remember vividly, she once remarked amongst colleagues in the department, how she sometimes woke up at 2am to mark exercise books for her classes. That left many of us agape with surprise. As Amy later remarked to me, "Surely, how many people wake up at 2 in the morning to mark books. Is it any wonder she's always banging on about exercise book trawling for marking and taking teachers to task? The poor woman needs to get a life, Kundai. She should get a life and a partner, instead of being work-obsessed and living by herself with her dog." Brutal stuff from Amy, but she was bang on in her estimation of Finicky's work-crazed idiosyncrasies.

As she upped her ante against me, I reckoned a diary would aid me most if I were subjected to constructive dismissal; I saw this for what it was and had once openly said to Finicky's face, "This is all about constructive dismissal, isn't it, Elaine? Isn't this all part of your desire to build up a sustained case against me, propped up by your lies that I am an incompetent teacher, devoid of classroom management skills, and should therefore be relived of my duties? I am an experienced English teacher; I am not a neophyte. And frankly, I don't need these hand-holding gestures of yours or being constantly shepherded all the time."

Finicky virulently rejected my accusation, saying, "Nothing could be further from the truth, Kundai. All I care about is the learning of the students. And I'm only trying to help you to become a better teacher, but it appears you've got the wrong end of the stick."

"Well, I respectfully disagree, Elaine. Your problem is, you have a perception that I am not a good teacher and that's where it ends; yours is a perception, as I've called it, and it is only in your mind. The reality, which is far removed from your perception, is, I'm a brilliant teacher, I know this, and the kids know this themselves. Otherwise, how do you account for my Media Studies classes being over-subscribed by students? And how is it you never give me credit for the high pass rate of students on my course?"

Predictably, Elaine let this one pass. She demurred, "I really do not want any conflict with you, Kundai, and was only trying to help." And with that, she was gone. But time and again, I found myself reflecting within myself, *why is it that fellow white teachers felt a black person needed to be helped all the time, as if they can't be trusted to be independent and competent concurrently?* After all, some of my colleagues, like Finicky, were still wet behind the ears and had only been teaching less than four years, a far cry from my vast experience and decades of secondary school teaching, for that matter, across two different cultural settings, England and Zimbabwe. Part of me felt this "white saviour" ideology didn't do anyone any good; it fed into yesteryear, racist, stereotype tropes of, "The nigger who needs to be constantly helped." I did not appreciate this condescending attitude and treatment in contemporary 21st Century Britain.

With time, I started logging some of my unsavoury experiences in the line of duty. One such entry which found its way in my diary ran thus:

> *Deputy Head of the School Jane Harper has been to see me today and questioned why I am bringing in Unions in the current matter involving myself and, "Developmental Teaching," as raised by Head of English Elaine Finicky (EFI). I've pointed out to Jane, I'm bringing in the Unions to protect myself. Jane went on to point out to me, "There's no need for you to have a meeting with Elaine and Union officials, as you requested. Instead, Geoff Essex, staff development manager, can have a meeting with you and he feeds back to Elaine."*

Looking back, I laugh at this brazen effort which was meant to stifle and intimidate me away from raising staff grievances against Elaine's tight-fisted rule and bullying shenanigans. Suffice to say, I steadfastly refused to go through an intermediary to speak to Elaine. I insisted any meeting with her had to be done with my Union representative present, which eventually only materialised without Elaine's presence, but with other senior leaders of the school; Elaine must have arm-twisted them and blatantly refused to attend. It was clearly palpable, so high and mighty was Elaine, she couldn't stomach being hauled to a restorative meeting with someone she considered as beneath her as I.

Some of the things I'm alluding to here may seem small, banal or trivial, but for one who had been subjected to, in some cases, veiled racism, it was abundantly clear racism was at play here. For instance, there was my eventual marginalisation from the English Department curriculum, whereby I couldn't be "allowed" to teach any other English groups above Year 9. Inwardly to myself, it was all laughable. *I am a trained English teacher, able to teach 11-18 age groups, not to mention my robust academic credentials in English.* But you know what? I was tired of trying to justify or explain myself to people who obviously had partial, preconceived bias against me. I knew I was competent and a brilliant professional, both in English and Media teaching, and I did not need the validation of someone who was inherently biased against me anyway. Once, when Elaine left and her sidekick Alison refused to line manage me over spurious reasons, I pretended to laugh over it, even though, inwardly, I saw it for what it was: the desire to not want to have anything to do with me because I was perceived to be a problem. I'm sure Alison had seen from my constant run-ins with her former boss Elaine, that she must have decided to not have anything to do with this fella. Alison was equally biased against me, just like her former boss Elaine. Each time Alison allocated English classes to me, she would find subtle ways to deprive me of those very classes, advancing very puerile reasons, such as, "As this is a shared class between you and I, I want to have more time with them. You can have the odd one-off lesson with them, in which you can consolidate other skills with them." This was another one of her perennial tactics with me, or she would dump me to the fancy called "accelerated reader programme," AR as we called it, in which I had to babysit English groups as they read in silence. Oft times, I used to chuckle at how Alison underestimated my intelligence, because I could see through the sheer façade of her underhanded shenanigans. These antics were meant to remove me from frontline English classroom teaching by marginalising me to odd, one-off English lessons or AR lessons. With a chuckle within myself, I used to liken my marginalisation from the English department under facile reasons, as my form of political Siberian banishment.

Then there was the absurd incident when Brackley School's Deputy Head, Jane Harper, summoned me to her office over allegations that I was a gangster. Yes, allegations that I was a gangster, ludicrous as it sounds. Apparently, according to Jane, some students had been going on about alleging, "Mr. Mafirakureva is a gangster who moves around with a knife in his pocket and he smokes weed." At first, I thought this was some sick joke. I couldn't believe a person as senior as a deputy head of a large comprehensive school would have the nerve to sit me down, an experienced member of staff, and spout such hogwash with a straight face. I politely refuted these assertions, which I found offensive, but it struck me Jane was not smart enough to realize the attendant undercurrents of associating black people with gangster culture.

There were always these seemingly small things which, as a person of colour, you do notice. And it's not as if I'm being overly sensitive. In most cases, Zet, my partner, concurred with me and characterised these seemingly "small" things as acts of covert racism and the perpetuation of white privilege. After all, here I was, leading a very successful Media Department, but without a financial acknowledgment of teaching and learning responsibility (TLR) to go with it. And in scenes reminiscent of my UPS1 threshold application at PRS, I had to approach the head, Simon Reece, to rightfully ask what other middle managers were getting. After much haggling and arm-twisting, Simon agreed to give me the lowest TLR on the scale!

Such is the black man's experience in English schools. I am not bitter, but I am clearly recounting my experiences for the over two decades I taught in English schools. It is only now, following the dreadful killing of George Floyd by police officers in Minneapolis in the United States in May 2020, that I feel brave enough to speak out against some injustices I experienced. As tragic as it is, George Floyd's cataclysmic death has given me a voice. I have found myself aligning more with the Black Lives Matter movement. I find that their discourse resonates with my desire to confront tyranny and social injustice in different spheres of life.

Even after arm-twisting Brackley Head Simon for a TLR allowance, and he agreed to award it, there was no official announcement or confirmatory public bulletin email. Such an announcement was generally the case with my fellow white colleagues each time Simon made new appointments or awarded them management allowances. Could I be taking things far and seeing whiteness in everything? No, I don't think so! It is ideal to call a spade a spade, for I can clearly see what's happening: The proverbial knee, which has been on the necks of me and others of my ilk for so long, was at it again.

Quite early on, I learned that belonging to a teacher's union was the best thing one could ever do as an ethnic minority teaching in English schools. Those quarterly teaching union subscriptions I paid was money well-spent, in the grand scheme of things. Simon the Head once quizzed me about why I needed to involve the union all the time, and I quipped, "With all due respect, sir, what you are asking me is akin to a judge enquiring why one needs a lawyer in court." That just about ended the conversation. I had a plethora of my teacher's union interventions following my many spats with Elaine Finicky, my over-exacting former Head of English. Many a time, teachers union intervention saved the day for me, retrieving me from the vagaries of well-orchestrated workplace bullying that was cleverly disguised under instituting accountability on my teaching practice.

Line management sessions with Finicky were an exercise in macabre torture, reminiscent of Frederick Fairlie's weird personality in Wilkie Collin's *Woman in White*. It was a self-aggrandising ego trip for Finicky, in which she tried to flex her muscles to me and show me she was in charge. I can relive the ghastly horrors of performance management sessions with her in trepidation, and how it must have given her the kicks to torment me with her unattainable targets. Time and again, I was made to feel I was less of an English teacher. Once, in fact, she tried to have me removed from the English Department under spurious charges, I fought tooth and nail out of my corner to prevent this. Eventually, Finicky relented and I lived to fight another day.

In clear cases of white privilege entrenched at Brackley and other schools where I taught in England, many a time I saw young, newly qualified white teachers and colleagues being promoted ahead of me. Yet some of them performed at a barely mediocre level on these jobs, which were clearly beyond their capabilities. But they were protected; they were part of the club. And you cannot say the black man is not seeing this. Some of the insights I gleaned during my long stint in teaching were: You had to be liked, your face had to fit within an establishment, or you remained on the fringes, like me. Looking back, there is no white privilege so palpable and prevalent as in the way promotions or appointments were made within schools like Brackley or PRS, where I taught. Had I been white, and had my face fit within a particular establishment, and given the number of teaching years' experience to my credit, by now, the highest position I would be enjoying would be an Assistant Headteacher. I say this from an informed position. I have observed my white colleagues who trained at similar times as me, or juniors who came after me several years later, all benefitted from the patronage appointments system and had been awarded far more senior leadership positions within schools, and clearly not on merit.

It is only now I have the courage to speak out boldly, calling out the culture of systemic racism and white privilege endemic within schools, thanks to the Black Lives Matter movement's high profile, "Get your knee off our neck" campaign. BLM has increasingly gained traction following the murder of George Floyd. Despite my professional expertise, experience, and competence, I have noticed in schools that the black man is treated as a lesser being who needs to be constantly chaperoned and needs handholding, the very evils I called out on my erstwhile line manager, Elaine Finicky.

It's not all been entirely a damp squib experience. There were some good moments, red letter day experiences, though largely isolated. I certainly miss Cynthia, my erstwhile head teacher, and her humane style of leadership laced with compassion. In 2010, my mother fell seriously ill in Zimbabwe. A colleague caught me in floods of tears, inconsolable, in my classroom cupboard. Mother's illness must have got to me and I let slip my carefully choreographed and well-guarded emotional mask. She had been unwell for some time. My heart sank as I feared for the worst. *Hadn't I lost my father in more or less similar circumstances, a decade earlier?* I reflected inwardly. *Perhaps it is Mother's swan song also, her final foray on this earth.* Cynthia allowed me to go and see my mother, in term time, at such a critical moment in my life, and for this gesture of limitless kindness, I am eternally grateful. What underlines Cynthia's kindness was, she permitted me to go and be with Mother at summer exam time, a key period in the school's calendar. Such was the depth and substance inherent in my pioneer boss, Ms. Grayling. What is more touching is, she did not tell me when to come back. It was more of a blank cheque compassionate leave, and inwardly, I made the right judgement call, two weeks away was just about reasonable.

A few weeks later, after my return from Zimbabwe, Cynthia summoned me to her office. "I just wanted to catch up with you, Kundai, and enquire about your mother's progress," she probed.

"She has made a phenomenal recovery, thank you," I responded, thanking Cynthia profusely. She wouldn't hear of my expressions of gratitude, though, and modestly brushed me aside.

"We have to look out after our staff, Kundai, the same way we look after our students. If we only emphasize the pastoral care of students, neglecting the adults, the staff, then we have failed," remarked Cynthia. I was visibly touched and moved by Cynthia's kindness. Years later, when she announced her retirement, it was a collective blow to myself and other staff, my colleagues. We all held Cynthia in high regard.

Cynthia had that rare personal connection with her staff which made it easier for mere mortals like me to feel at ease with her. She always had that knack of knowing the idiosyncrasies of her staff, which meant both general conversation or small talk were easier with her, even though she was our boss. We chatted a lot about Zimbabwe and South Africa, as she showed a keen interest in where I came from. When I wrote my MA thesis based on Zimbabwe, she personally requested a copy, which she read, and we had lengthy discussions on it. I guess I have so much nostalgia and reverence for my former boss, who was one who helped give me a footing in the English educational sector, something I noted on her huge staff farewell card, upon her retirement from Brackley School.

CHAPTER 14

Ghost of Finicky Resurrected

Two years following Finicky's departure, my erstwhile, over-exacting head of department, I found myself dealing with yet another bully, Ms. Muriel Finister. She oversaw BTEC courses delivery at The Brackley School. For the uninitiated, BTEC courses are vocational qualifications which are irredeemably dumbed-down so they could appeal to kids, though in reality, it did not always translate to that. In addition, most schools tended to favour BTECs over traditional, conventional courses like normal GCSEs and A Levels. The assumption was, BTECs were easy fodder, which could translate into students attaining huge passes and thus bump up the overrated English school performance league tables. So, far from the fiction peddled by school authorities, BTECs had nothing to offer students, other than an arid, insipid, exceedingly uninspiring, intellectually dry curriculum, whose only *raison d'etre* was at the behest of glorifying individual schools in national ratings and English league tables' glory. Add to that, the voluminous amount of needless paperwork which had to be completed by both teachers and students, as part of the coursework submission for this dinosaur qualification. Then it completed the crumbling edifice. It was an open secret there was no academic substance to this BTEC qualification, notwithstanding the over-the-top hype to the contrary by the school authorities.

"It's like the exam board knows their qualification is crap, and this needless paperwork is a facile attempt to justify their useless qualification that we're a force to reckon with." Many a time, I had pointed this out to colleagues alike, who shared similar sentiments as I, and were skeptical and derisive of BTEC qualifications. But what could we mere mortals do? We had no power to resist delivering these mundane, archaic, anachronistic courses, and were usually at the mercy of draconian school authorities' rolling juggernaut: "You either deliver this course, or there will be no teaching place for you at this school. BTECSs is the way we are going now." This was a threat which wasn't taken lightly, given how the Covid-19 pandemic had made it increasingly difficult to switch jobs or get another job. So, in the end, teachers like me who had put up a protracted, spirited resistance steadfastly refusing to teach BTECs ended up buckling to the hegemony's pressure and acquiescing to teaching the dreaded BTEC, instead. That was how it came to be that I crossed paths with wily Ms. Muriel Finister, teacher in charge of BTECs.

Ms. Finister reminded me of my earlier nemesis at PRS, Jacky Pinhead, in that both were power-crazed megalomaniacs whose aphrodisiac was all out power against all odds. They both took sadistic pleasure in "terrorising" subordinates, especially men. On our first meeting, Muriel ensured she was straight with me that she was gunning for the school's ultimate prize, the headship. And in her words, Simon Reece, the current head "better watch out for me. You see me, Kundai, I am 37 now, and by 40, I see myself in charge of this school, no two ways about it. I have the experience, charisma, traction and what it takes." She spoke through her goofy teeth, bobbing her head sideways, eyes darting to and fro as if she were trying to hypnotize me with her naked ambition. Seeing as Simon, the current head, was in no hurry to leave his post soon, it occurred to me what a delusional goober she was!

"I see," I remarked at such brazenness with a subordinate on a first meeting, yet she carried on, unperturbed by me.

Ms. Finister announced, "My BTEC empire has grown incredibly at this school because of me, my efforts; I have done a lot for the school. About time I get my due recognition. And what better way to fulfil this than to become head of Brackley?"

I had a clear sense of déjà vu. Even as she spoke, it would not be long before I fell out with this woman, twittering on before me about her misplaced sense of self-importance. The first signs of our falling out came on much earlier than I had anticipated.

Time and again, I had these run-ins with some of these weird characters. I found my thoughts wandering to James Baldwin's words in his famous 1965 Cambridge University student union address: "Is the American dream at the expense of the American negro?" Only this time, I couldn't help flipping that to, *"Are British immigrants' lesser beings than their fellow citizens, even some of us who were now fellow citizens, following our naturalization?"* I was tired of the trite way people of my ilk were treated within English schools, and of the condescending attitude and relentless put downs from junior fellow teachers like Finister, whose trite racism, among a litany of other subtle forms of bullying, plagued our lot. What got to me was how this brazen, systematic behaviour tended to be visited only upon fellow black teachers; even non-academic staff in the school's employ were not spared either.

Jason, one amiable chap, was literally hounded out of Brackley School by Finister's bullying shenanigans, and in the end, he willingly threw in the towel. "I am tired of all this bullshit, Kundai. This morning I approached Simon, the head, and tendered my resignation. After Christmas, I'm out of here, mate," Jason remarked to me, with the air of a defeated and subjugated being. I said to him, "But are you sure you're not running away from your shadow Jason? Because wherever you go, whichever school you move onto in England, you will come across this systematic bullying and intimidation of staff. Why don't you stay put here and fight from your corner, like I've done over my two-decades stint here?"

"I just told you I'm tired and done with Finister's antics, didn't I? It's too much, and it is affecting my health and even my home life. I can't even get a hard on anymore with my wife! And now, that's not fair to her. There has to be somewhere out there where things are better than this hell hole, and for want of a cliché, to add insult to injury, this is flipping BTEC we're talking of here," Jason commiserated. "It's not like BTEC is some super subject, but what does Finister do? She tries to make out that BTEC is some super-duper physics aerodynamics science!"

"Well, you have to know insecure people do that a lot; they're hopelessly out of their depth. So, to cover their insecurities and inadequacies, they have these unjustified delusions of grandeur they exhibit through needless bullying, as in her case. It's all an ego-centric power trip with Muriel. In that respect, she reminds me of my ex-wife, actually," I replied. Then I added, "Finister is vacuous and vapid. There's nothing up there in comparison to Finicky my yester-year tormentor. Finicky had some brains and intelligence, I'll give her that, though a bully is a bully, regardless of whether they're smart or not."

Later on, that evening, in the quiet solitude of my abode, I found my thoughts wandering to my conversation with good old Jason. It was not only Jason who had been at the receiving end of this abrasive culture and system at The Brackley School. Kofi, my Ghanaian friend and professional colleague, had suffered a similar fate; he had been denied a pay raise on flimsy charges that his classroom management skills weren't up to standard. They had brazenly told him, "You see Kofi, the kids are constantly complaining, there isn't much learning going on in your lessons, so we have to take these concerns seriously." Geoff, the school staff development manager, had patronisingly relayed the Sword of Damocles to my hapless friend Kofi.

On hearing this, I countered, "And why didn't you challenge it?" I was visibly aghast, and a tad exasperated, by my friend's inaction. I chided him, "Do you have to be that placid all the time?"

"But, what else could I say? I have a wife and three kids to take care of, not to mention my stifling mortgage bill every month. Would you pay my mortgage if I get the sack?" he countered menacingly towards me. I understood him, I understood Kofi's dejection and defeat. Had we all not been there before? Walked that proverbial, familiar road, where one became a slave of family responsibilities which, in a way, exacerbated our exploitation and abuse.

After what seemed an eternity, he resumed speaking, "They've put me under a teacher support programme."

"Teacher support programme, oh my word! That's the commencement of capability procedure process, Kofi," I said. "Why on earth would you agree to such a preposterous move? It's akin to signing your professional death warrant," I told him, bluntly and blatantly.

"Once again, Kundai, you talk as if I hold the levers of power. Can't you see I am emasculated in all this? Geoff has me firmly held by the balls this time."

"And what if you refuse?"

"Refuse? There's nothing like refusing a directive from the school head, and Geoff made it succinctly clear, he was acting with the head's full blessings."

I angrily retorted, "Well, they may as well both go to hell. Now let me level with you here, Kofi. I am not about to let them wrest your qualified teacher status away from you, just like that, at their calling, at the drop of a hat. Do you hear me? Goodness knows, we suffered enough to get this QTS in the first place."

"But...but...what are my options, I ask again," stammered Kofi.

"Well, you can exercise the right not to be unilaterally stripped of your teaching qualification, at someone's whims and fancies.

I'll tell you one good tip we got from our Oxford tutors during teacher training: If you ever find yourself being put under capability procedure, then that's the time to jump, before you're pushed. I would resign, mate, of my own volition, then look for a job at another school."

I continued, "I tell you, Kofi, once you allow them to screw you by taking your QTS via the backdoor, put you on capability, then you're finished, professionally that is, as a teacher here in England. With capability written all over you, on your CV, you may as well kiss goodbye to secondary school teaching ever again in England. No school would touch you ever again! So, I am saying, you check-mate them; it's a game of wits, Kofi. He who dares, wins. For goodness sake you should watch *The Queen's Gambit,* at some point, so you stay clued up, mate, on how to be always one step ahead of your opponents!"

Kofi went dead quiet for a couple of minutes. I could see he was reflecting, flicking through his mind, reflecting on what I had just said to him, as if looking for options. Then he said, "Fine, Kundai, thank you for this, mate; I know I stress a lot about my filial and family responsibilities, but what are my options, if I can never teach again because of this capability, procedure thing? Over this weekend I will speak with my wife Jenny, and I should offer my resignation immediately, just so I can stave off stillbirth to my professional career. Goodness knows, like you, I've worked so hard through teacher training to get QTS, only to let it slip through my fingers, just like that."

"Way to go, mate," I quietly acquiesced. "In the meantime, you can register as a supply teacher with many of the teaching agencies. That's a stop gap measure. It keeps the bills paid till you secure a much more permanent contract. It's a win-win situation for you; you retain your QTS for life, and you won't let these fuckers screw you ad infinitum."

In no time, after tendering his resignation, Kofi left The Brackley School, which caught the school leadership team completely off-guard. "Can you imagine, Geoff tried persuading me to stay on, but I stuck to my guns. It's time to move to pastures anew, Geoff, I believe I've done my bit here," I said.

That was it, the black man's lived experience in Britain was always the politics of survival, in which one sought to protect oneself, always being ten steps ahead of one's perceived "tormentors." In a weird way, it made me think of the Corleone family saga of the famed *Godfather* trilogy, and how Michael Corleone was always one step ahead of his adversaries. And so, Kofi, Jason, and I always had to be ahead of our detractors. Patrick, a friend of mine, a university lecturer amongst one of the Russell groups unis, gave it a name: "working whilst black."

Drawing on my personal experience in various English schools whereI have taught, I painfully realised black people were pigeonholed at the workplace. I had noticed a dual dichotomy in which black people were consigned. In other words, there are two kinds of black people at the workplace. Those who are given a veneer of responsibility to show some semblance of inclusion and those who do not and are left to suffer whilst the former are allowed to go through the ranks for box ticking optics purposes to the outside world that we are an equal opportunities employer, a fact most schools liked to flaunt at interviews or on their websites that they meet this particular aspect.

In reflective mode, following the untimely but strategic departure of my friend, Kofi, I reminisced drawing on my personal experience and that of other black teachers how things were nigh hard for us in English classrooms. As a black teacher, I found my professionalism and competence were constantly judged, put under microscopic gaze, and maligned by junior teachers, some who joined the profession way after me. Aside from my egregious dealings with PRS's Jacky Pinhead and Finicky later at Brackley, I was to later have further bruising with Muriel Finister, the BTEC overlord, as I called her.

A dwarf of a woman, with an annoyingly staccato voice, Muriel certainly had delusions of grandeur the way she threw her weight about at The Brackley School, banging on nonstop about her being the saviour of the school, courtesy of her "flourishing" BTEC grades. She joined the usual beneficiary of the patronage appointment system, which saw incompetent people being awarded positions of leadership because of their servile obsequiousness and sycophancy. I had the unfortunate displeasure of dealing with her as the BTEC overlord. Once, at the start and commencement of BTEC assignments, she had to check the paperwork of my Media course and to moderate it, even though she had the barest minimal subject knowledge of the course, which in the end adversely impacted our professional working relationship.

From my professional dealings with her, it was patently palpable that Muriel was hopelessly out of her depth with the subject knowledge of my course, Media Studies, yet she attempted to throw about her unfettered weight and exert undue influence on me, as what happened that fateful Wednesday afternoon, when I met up with her to moderate scripts for my Year 11 GCSE Media class. A moderation meeting should not exceed an hour, but with this self-styled BTEC overlord, the meeting ended up degenerating into a farcical marathon meeting. We were both quibbling on semantics, as I tried to put Muriel right for daring to trash my judicious marking and student's brilliant work, which she valiantly failed to discern and acknowledge because the subject knowledge eluded her. As such, she ended up exhibiting her obtuseness. "But you haven't met the brief, Kundai," she charged at me, a triumphant *got 'ya* smile, curling her rotund, pugnacious face.

"But I have met the coursework brief," I countered her baseless charges. "How have I not met the brief? Can you please clarify, Muriel?"

"Well, the task is a skill and evidence based, and your students haven't demonstrated any skills," she alleged.

"In what way have they not demonstrated any skills? As you can see from Chrissy's folder here, she has an array of activities done, which in actual fact, showcases her wide repertoire of skills and techniques gained thereof," I replied.

"Well, they shouldn't have created a mood board," Muriel claimed. "What skills does that show? Nothing, no skills whatsoever!"

"A mood board shows planning skills," I replied. "It demonstrates how an idea can be formulated, from conception, where it's brainstormed, till full realization. And looking closely at said brief, it clearly states, in unequivocal language, that one of the outcomes for the assignment is a practical object."

"But there are no skills demonstrated here." The back-and-forth trudged on unabated.

"What about the audience research inherent in these portfolios?"

"It's not about audience research, Kundai. What has audience got to do with skills? This is malpractice; it's quite serious. You haven't met the exam board brief here," she droned on, in her insipid voice.

"I'm afraid you're wrong, Muriel, and I respectfully disagree with you, here. Awareness of target audience is key in any development of media production. There is no way one can proceed to make and develop a media production without awareness of who it's meant for. Otherwise, what's the point of producing it then?"

Finister shifted awkwardly in her chair at this. I could see she wasn't yet done with me and was not going to give up in her put downs of me and how I had, in her opinion, cocked up the kids' important Media course by failing to interpret the coursework brief, as she put it.

"What else?" I remarked impatiently at her. Then she picked up the coursework brief again and looked at it intently, after which she remarked in her annoyingly sonorous voice, "It says here on the brief, you're not supposed to produce a production, and yet you have let your students produce two magazine covers. This is wrong, Kundai. You have missed the coursework brief requirements."

"Once again, I respectfully disagree with you Muriel. Your reading of the brief is clearly different from mine and we're now just wasting time, quibbling on semantics. The brief clearly states, students should work on producing a finished product, refined in the post-production phase, and if you can't get this, then I'm afraid I will defer this matter to an independent second opinion," I remarked, as I made to stand up, indicating my frustration with her dimness, but she wasn't going to let me go just like that, not without being deliberately awkward again.

"Well, you can ask anyone for all you like, but you're wrong, I've been running these BTEC courses for quite some time now, and I know what I'm talking about here. I am the ultimate fountain of wisdom and knowledge, as far as BTEC courses are concerned." she said with a dismissive flourish of the hand.

I must admit, for someone woefully out of her depth, Finister had a "smart" mouth! She was certainly a dandy talker, given her dearth of Media subject knowledge. Her voice grated on me each time she spoke, not to mention her annoying smirk, which reminded me of odious Priti "Awful" Patel. I was beginning to get increasingly annoyed with all this hogwash, so, I gave it back in equal measure. I said, "But with all due respect, Muriel, you do not have monopoly on knowledge. In any case, you fail to see this is something way beyond your own subject knowledge. I can't claim to know your designated subject area Biochemistry in the same way. You shouldn't purport to be an expert on my subject, Media Studies. Why don't you stay in your lane, and I stay in mine?"

She must have come psyched up to fight that day, for she then whacked out a supposedly video tutorial from her desk, on which she attempted to patronisingly define the terms, "production" and "post-production" to me. But I was not going to give her any further leeway. As it was, she'd already eaten and wasted a significant chunk of my time.

"You know what, Muriel, I've just about had enough of this tittle-twaddle. Respective of other people's views, you and I are not going to agree on this, simply on a matter of parlance. I've already said this before. I will get a second opinion on this and get back to you." With that I mumbled my goodbyes and brusquely left. That was just about how I managed to escape from Muriel's clutches that day, but a meeting which had started at roughly two-thirty in the afternoon had dragged on to roughly ten-to-six in the evening, all for the love of someone's grandiose, power-crazed psyche.

It took me having to speak to other senior colleagues within the school to check my folder of work, which Finister had trashed for them, to right the situation. Actually, they told her to "sod off," as my work was in order, and if anything, I had done due diligence and adhered to the exam board requirements to the letter, contrary to Muriel's far-fetched notions that I had cocked things up, and my malfeasance would invite the wrath of malpractice to the school. But as is usually the case with bullies, Finister smarted at this public humiliation, or dressing down, as she perceived it. She started a war of attrition in which she, like her predecessor Finicky, deployed email surveillance to orchestrate her bullying antics and shenanigans against me to higher levels. It was at the peak of my frustration with these silly mind games and trivia that a brilliant idea spawned in me. It was an exit strategy, which came with me applying for a part-time PhD degree with Birmingham City University, which I had secretly decided to embark on. The plan was, in time, this would be my exit strategy from the rigmarole of mundane secondary school teaching, pedantry, and its unrealistic demands.

Like my fellow African brethren who had jumped ship earlier, I, too, felt my time was nigh and fast approaching. I had done my bit in secondary school teaching, and post-PhD, I saw another world beckoning.

I digress and revert to cyber-bullying, an oft-used tool amongst ourselves as fellow professional teachers. Email was a powerful weapon mostly employed to bully black teachers into servile, acquiescing submission and humiliation, denigrating them that they were, "numpties" or "dimwits," who didn't really know what they were doing, and thus needed the proverbial white saviour syndrome to hold their guiding hands. I remember this too well; I had lived through this ordeal, seen it a lot visited on myself, from the Finicky days to now the Muriel Finister era; Muriel now perfected and notched it up a scale further. This modus operandi was not surprising; it was a befitting stereotype and ideology which aligned itself well with the "black people as children perspective," long replicated in racist colonial discourses, and peddled in diverse forms of media, from time immemorial. Muriel would deploy her email arsenal with sadistic, vindictive glee, as she attempted to humiliate and dress me down, putting me down by unnecessarily carbon copying emails to me to other senior members of staff within the school in her attempts to soil my professionalism and cast aspersions on it. Each time she tried these silly games, I squared up to her, just as I had done with my earlier tormentor Finicky. And one day, in a dramatic turn of events, the staffroom was abuzz with an excited state of gossip and chatter, as everyone whispered, "Oh, have you heard, Kundai?"

"Heard what?" I remarked, oblivious of the seismic changes which were about to unfold.

"Well, well, Kundai, you're surely the last to know in town. Ms. High and Mighty Finister just handed in her notice upstairs," they remarked, gesturing towards the stairs, as the school's administration was housed in the second-floor building.

"Really?" I remarked incredulously. "How is this? Isn't it, BTECs was her fiefdom, and she would never leave until she got the ultimate Brackley prize, headship?" I chuckled mischievously, a wicked glint in my eyes.

"Well, that's the paradox, Kundai. She applied for the deputy headship post, which she flunked in the interview, and in typical, fuzzy goo fashion, she's thrown her toys from the pram."

"Good riddance! About time, too!" gleefully shouted someone across the staffroom.

I decided to keep my thoughts to myself on Muriel's departure, but it's not untrue to say I wouldn't miss her a bit.

Looking back and taking stock of my professional relationship, inwardly, there were times I wish I should have verbalized my frustration with these charlatans. Barring professionalism constraints, I should have told them right to their bovine faces, "Forget about your misplaced, white supremacist, racist bullshit. You know what? I'm a smart nigger! Get used to that. I will not let you get away with your thinly veiled bigotry, trampling on my inalienable rights as you lot did yester-year with our forefathers. In any case, I equally draw inspiration from those heroes of yester-year. Thus today, I valiantly declare, we are all Rosa Park!"

CHAPTER 15

Brackley Diaries – The Other Side

On the plus side, I had some good friendships with a wide repertoire of the staff at Brackley; some staff members were genuine and friendly colleagues, like Jo Waverly, my esteemed NQT mentor, who has also remained another longstanding loyal friend to this day. Sarah was another close, personal friend, as was affable librarian Sue Velma, "The Vicar of Dimbleby," as I called her, and my next-door neighbor, as her library was housed next to my media classroom. Sue also doubled up as my surrogate mother. And there was Amy, my esteemed union rep, who valiantly fought from my corner, tooth and nail, during the Finicky years. To Amy, "Thank you, mate, I never got to give you a proper send off."

Then there was quirky Dr, Roylott, the controversial poet and colleague from the English Department, with whom I got along so well and constantly enjoyed sparring on contemporary politics in Britain, all in good banter, of course. Once I was poignantly moved by Roylott's kindness when he offered me support and pledged to sit in a meeting with me during the dark days of Elaine Finicky's reign of terror. It was, at that time, and it made me realize whom one could count on to fight from their corner or stand with one in solidarity in the face of adversity.

In looking back, I am very delighted to have interacted with Roylott; he was always fired up and in top form in our robust exchanges on matters political and mundane. Once we argued over the Dominic Cummings furore, when the latter allegedly flouted the lockdown measures in the first wave of the Covid-19 pandemic. Then, Roylott was on another level, as he fiercely defended Cummings, and I equally gave it back, sticking to my guns. Roylott remarked, "I hope you don't take this the wrong way, Kundai, but this is my viewpoint: a man is being hounded here, lynched by both the public and an acquiescing leftie media, for daring to look out after his wife and dyslexic child." Roylott went on, venting his exasperation, "Did you see how the sodding media have staked out his London house? Oh, my word, what for?" Can you imagine if it was the other way round, what your side would be saying at this level of harassment?"

I replied, "But I respectfully disagree, Roylott, I'm afraid it's not as simplistic as you are making it out to be. Cummings is a lying weasel who thinks he knows it all, and by flouting Covid lockdown rules, which everyone else, the great British public, are following, I'm afraid he's crossed the red line here, especially as he's the establishment's top decision maker or spin doctor, if you prefer the term. The man has to go, Roylott, whatever you say. Cummings' position is no longer tenable; the man has stuck his two fingers to all of us who've been religiously following the lockdown measures to the letter."

"Of course not, Kundai, don't be ridiculous and melodramatic about all this. Cummings' position is not untenable in any way. I disagree with you there."

We lived to fight another duel, as our views failed to reach consensus on the Cummings Gate scandal. Still, I got along with Roylott; we never let our differences in political outlook or perception stand in the way. Such was the depth and testament of my friendship with eccentric Roylott.

At times we would have fiery exchanges on Brexit, with Roylott calling me out, "You lot and your side don't want to accept you've lost the argument here, let alone the referendum result which you don't want to acknowledge." This always fascinated me, how he framed our verbal sparring, couching them in this binary opposite *Us versus Them* dichotomy.

"But that's preposterous Roylott," I shot back. "You know very well I'm a democrat and I have grudgingly accepted the referendum results. Anything else to the contrary is hogwash. In fact, nothing could be further from the truth; when we call out the Leave campaign's lies, pre-vote deceit, their well-choreographed chicanery, and propaganda, it's because of sour grapes mindset."

"So says a Re-moaner democrat," quipped Roylott in his typical sarcastic fashion. There was no offence meant; it was all done tongue-in-cheek, as was the nature of our amity.

We had a great friendship growing with Roylott, a relationship punctuated by mutual respect for the divergence and differences of opinion we both shared in our political outlook and wider perspectives. Perhaps our other affinity was consolidated by our mutual, shared love and appreciation for literature and writing. The prodigious poet and writer he was, Roylott would share with me his creative pieces, and likewise, I would bounce my creative output off him. Once, I had a piece on Michelle Obama's *Becoming* memoir published, and upon being congratulated by another member of staff, I brushed her aside trying to be modest, all within Roylott's earshot of course, who gleefully retorted, "Come on, Kundai, stop this humble brag thing, just accept it and get on with it."

"What are you on about, mate, what's a humble brag?" I sheepishly remarked amidst trying to suppress a chuckle.

"A humble brag, that's typical you, vintage Kundai, trying, pretending, to be modest, at the same time, basking and crowing in your personal glory. Just accept it, mate, without all this modesty bullshit."

"Haha, I don't know what you're on about," I laughed off his remarks.

Then there was an interesting coincidence in how we both

idolized, venerated, Dickens and Wilkie Collins as great writers, though we could never actually agree on the latter's greatest text, pitting *The Moonstone* vis-a-vis *The Woman in White.*

"*The Woman in White* does it for me, Roylott, what a sublime story! Count Fosco, the Napoleonic master criminal, the formidable Marian Halcombe, resolute Walter Hartright, the drawing master, Madame Fosco, the obsequious Countess, with such breathtaking loyalty towards her husband, how can I ever forget such larger-than-life characters? You gotta give it to *Woman in White,* Roylott."

"Well, I get that, but I respectfully disagree. I will always go with *The Moonstone.* Whatever you say, Kundai, *The Moonstone* is one of the greatest detective crime stories of all times. In fact, it can well be the forebearer of present-day crime drama texts, and Wilkie Collins did a brilliant job for that matter by setting the bar very high."

Roylott and I also enjoyed Dickens' *Our Mutual Friend* and *Bleak House*, among other greats, revelling in Dickens' wit at creating such memorable, enduring characters as Caroline, (Caddy) in *Bleak House.* Caddy, Mrs. Jellyby's daughter of telescopic philanthropic infamy; 'I'm pen and ink to Ma,' whined poor Caddy, as she sat dwarfed by the vast swathes of paper and ink as her mother undertook global charity to greater heights, the brazen irony lost on her, how her own large family was wanting in the very charity she was dispensing beyond the borders."

Both Roylott and I laughed and shared a common bond on this sardonic Dickensian humour, or his lampooning of the legal system, be it in *Great Expectations*, through Jaggers and Wemmick's portraits, or *Bleak House,* through the notorious, long drawn out Jarndyce and Jarndyce lawsuit in the decaying Court of Chancery Lane in London, or Dickens taking pot shots at a dry, mechanical educational system, highlighted through the grotesque portrayal of Bradley Headstone, the school master in *Our Mutual Friend.* We certainly had a blast, my mate and I.

There's an interesting back story to the moniker Roylott, for Roylott is not actually my learned colleague's real name, which I will, however, not seek to reveal. Interestingly, the name Roylott was borne out of both our adulation of Sir Arthur Conan Doyle's detective fiction stories, in particular *The Speckled Band*, a short story we taught our junior English classes, Years 8 and 9. In the story in question is an eccentric, enigmatic character, Dr. Grimesby Roylott, known for his erratic behaviour and volatile temper, which made him run Stoke Moran Manor, his countryside residence, with an ironclad fist. In fact, so feared was Dr. Roylott that he hardly kept any domestic staff, and legend had it, back in his heydays in India, he had given his butler a terrible "hiding," with tragic consequences for the unfortunate "little devil!" My very own friend Roylott could paint a searing, vivid, graphic description of this pantomime villain. Not only that, but he could also perform an uncanny impression of Roylott's voice, and to celebrate our enduring enjoyment of Sherlock Holmes' stories, Dr. Roylott he became, to this day.

In equal measure, I had a rewarding and fulfilling professional relationship and personal friendship with my first ever head of English, Roland Kinnock, the man who mentored me. *The Kinnock Years*, so named after Roland's last name, are equally worthy of mention, as Roland and I developed a genuine, respectful camaraderie which has lasted to this very day. The name Kinnock also made for good banter between us, as we were characterised "lefties," by some of our sixth form students, due to our perceived political leanings and affiliation. In general terms, I had wide-ranging personal experiences in my over two-decade stint in English schools.

Among other allies within the wider school, were also the inimitable members of the PE, Art and RS Departments, who always made me feel welcome; there were times I felt like PE, Art and RS were my other habitat, as well. By and large, these decent beings were able to, in some cases, voice and privately share their disgust with me, particularly in relation to how people of my ilk were treated by the school's hegemony. Others were more vociferous in their condemnation. "I salute you, all my fellow colleagues. This narrative is in equal measure yours also, where I get to acknowledge and laud your selfless humanity and decency for professional lives well-lived, as we all answered the call to our vocation attending to those broken lives, mending them, nurturing the nation's human resources, those youngsters whom we've done right by."

CHAPTER 16

And Then There was Mrs. Hudson, et al

It would be amiss not to acknowledge and celebrate my key constituency, those who made me to be where I am today, my students. In looking back at my teaching career, spanning over two decades, none gives me greater happiness and professional fulfilment than I derive from the excellent rapport I had with my students over the years. Never mind that the *classroom management* misnomer phrase was constantly shoved in my face as a whipping tool to bash me and stifle my self-esteem. I have had an excellent mutual understanding with the generality of the students I taught. Some of my more honest colleagues called it charisma on my part. I don't know about that one. I won't blow my trumpet on this one, but I can attest, I did get along well with most of the students I taught in the different English schools where I worked, particularly Brackley, where I became something of a local celebrity with both students, parents, and the local community. The positive end result of this was that I presided over a Media Department, with brilliant academic results over a sustained number of years to warrant Ofsted commendation in 2012, at a time Brackley School was in special measures.

Most of my students fared very well in national exams, in higher education, and have become distinguished leaders and experts in the different fields they ventured into. One unique tenet of my relationship with the kids was the nicknames galore I gave them, and they gave it back in equal measure. I have lost count of the litany of nicknames I gave them, which perhaps consolidated the harmony with my students. I was nonetheless a stickler for upholding professional standards and did not hesitate to crack the proverbial whip if students ever stepped out of line. I stayed true to the ethos of my practice, maintaining professional boundaries to the letter. I took wisdom from Oxford University teacher training classes, where our tutors used to drum into us, "When you go out there to teach in the classrooms, be aware that you will always be the adult in that room, and they are kids. Kids will remain kids, and so if a situation arises, you are the adult in the room. Make or take that all-important decision befitting of a professional and responsible adult." And I could say I pretty much stuck to this advice, which I adopted as the general rule of thumb with my classes. Even though we had moments of fun and laughter, I ensured they learnt well in my lessons.

Much of the nomenclature derived from our Media Studies curricula, the wide repertoire of films and television drama shows we studied in class. There was Mrs. Hudson, that is brilliant Natasha, who has successfully forged a media career as a digital media consultant and entrepreneur, and so, named after the quirky Mrs. Hudson, Sherlock's eccentric 221B Baker Street landlady and housekeeper, in the iconic BBC Sherlock Holmes tv show. Then I had Brangellina and Pablito, that is Steph and Jason from the famed class of 2017 legends. What lasting memories I have enjoyed with my media classes over the years. Who can forget our media trips, ranging from the BBC Television Centre trips in London, where we did a *Dr. Who* role play, and those playful sessions sitting on Blue Peter set, the Warner Bros. Studio tour in London, the Los Angeles and New York jaunts inter alia? Some students remarked how they got their confidence boosted from these trips and it influenced their future career choices. I know for sure Harry has become a successful TV producer for renowned British public service free-to-air television network Channel 4. He has also produced flagship television drama shows for streaming giant Netflix. David, or Sam Mendes, as I called him, is a film director of note with infinite sublime productions to come. Phil *"The Bottle"* is a published author as we speak, with his acclaimed debut novel, Cows Can't Jump. These are but a few of my erstwhile students who have made it out there in the world. And nothing gives me greater pleasure than to celebrate their success.

The interesting things about the nicknames bandied around between teacher and students was usually my getting caught out on parents' evenings when I had some momentary blips in which I forgot some of the students' real names, much to the amusement of the parents, as the kids would try to help me out by whispering their real names under their breaths in low tones. They say legends never die. I believe that is true of some of the best brains I taught in Brackley at the Brackley School. Owing to the strength and diversity of these brilliant minds, it is difficult to list all of them here, but suffice to say, certain cohorts are conspicuous and thus merit pointing out. Class of 2012/13 A Level Media deserve special mention, as it's the first time ever it happened on my course that I was oversubscribed with students wanting to take the course at A Level. So, the timetable committee had to cater for two Media groups. Now, this is big, a huge feat, because at A Level these are optional courses and when students elected to pick your course, it felt like a positive endorsement of one's teaching prowess, or a popularity contest, as my esteemed colleague Roylott put it.

How can I forget that brilliant cohort, names like Phil *"The Bottle,"* Alex *JFC*, George *Alan Shearer,* among others comes to mind. Such brilliant and talented youngsters. Class of 2017/18 also stands out for similar reasons; that was of the Brangellina, Steph, Jordan, Nosey Parker Junior, also known as Kirsten, Michelle Obama, *DCI Cloth* Megan, Emma, Amba, Lily, Quigley, Hollie, Melissa, Broccoli, and Tom of *Lady Gaga* fame, among others. There are far too many to mention here, but you are all held in high esteem. I salute you all. I have immortalized you in the BCC Media Hall of Fame in recognition of your stellar work.

I have enjoyed the laughter though, when my students have given back the classroom banter to me, parroting some of my mundane sayings back to me. How can I forget Shannon *Motormouth* and her in jest impressions of me: *"I'm working hard, Sir, I'm thoroughly ashamed of myself, Sir, you've taught us well. Complacency is the downfall of many a many."* Shannon was able to do all this, valiantly trying to capture my accent, all in good humour, which she lamentably failed to replicate. I was equally chuffed when she eventually went on to study film and media at university. It's been hilarious reminiscing on those wonderful classroom moments.

My teaching days were never dull or short of drama, both at PRS and Brackley, with my coterie of students. A typical day would range from the mundane to the melodramatic, all in one fell swoop.

"Sir, can you teach us your Zimbabwe language?" quipped Maya.

"There is no one Zimbabwe language to talk of," I replied with a straight face, "but we have several languages which count as indigenous languages ranging from Shona, Ndebele, Venda, Kalanga, and although I speak fluent Shona, I am not proficient in the other languages, as I am from the Manyika tribe, though I hate the word 'tribe,' especially its negative, stereotypical connotations to non-whites. But anyway, that's beside the point. As a *Manyika, Samanyika* as my clansmen call me, we hail from Eastern, Zimbabwe, Manicaland province to be precise, and I grew up in the provincial capital, Mutare city," I said, with a lot of undisguised pride to my students.

"As a Manyika, I am exceedingly proud of my Shona heritage and our distinctive, heavy accent, which was the butt of many uncouth jokes at university. When I was at the University of Zimbabwe, other fellow students, particularly those from Harare, used to take the mickey on my Manyika accent. Then I could get offended, but now I am ever so proud of my identity."

"Okay, sir, how do you say 'hello' in Shona or Manyika? Please just tell us," implored Jaden, one of the naughty students.

"Okay, anyone interested in learning my Shona language, see me during lunch. I will have all the time in the world to tutor you," I said with a peremptory wave of my hand to keep the class quiet. "I know your tricks, but you're here to…"

"We're here to LEARN!" bellowed all the students in deafening unison, drowning me out in my typical accent, as they knew I was wont to say.

"Okay, okay, glad you now know my requirements as your teacher," I chuckled with another wave of hand, as I did my usual round of the class, checking on their work.

Oftentimes, it would be another kid, telling off a fellow student for daring to disrupt the lesson, as tended to happen with my bottom set, Year 8 English class. "Shut up, Kessia, we're trying to learn! Can't you see the man is trying to teach us English?" remarked Tom one afternoon, one of the conscientious lads in the class, after which he graciously resumed. "Sir, I'm grateful to you for teaching us, I know what I know because of you," he would say. Teaching had its moments; it was edifying and sweet to get such endorsement from the kids. I couldn't resist a chuckle and coy smile at this; my students could be very sweet, when they chose. "Thank you, Tom," I modestly acknowledged his compliment, as we proceeded to have a productive lesson that afternoon.

Such was the rapport and camaraderie with my classes. Sometimes I would relent and teach them bits and bobs of phrases in my Shona language. The more daring would try to say "good morning" or "good afternoon" in my vernacular. Next time they saw me, and because it was hilarious when they tried to mimic my accent, they got it horribly wrong, which triggered more laughter from me. Then, at times, like this particular morning, I had to make the right judgement call on whether these seeming interests in my culture and language were not just clever, time wasting techniques to detract from learning English, which some of them used to diss.

"I hate English, Sir."

"Why do we have to learn about Shakespeare or Dickens, people who died long ago? What good is it to any of us present day teenagers? I mean, how is this even relevant to my life bruv?" These were typical questions from some of my students, and this always inwardly hurt and pricked me through, their lack of appreciation of greats like Dickens and Wilkie Collins, personal favourites of mine. For someone who venerated Dickens' literature and contribution, I had to be at pains to explain the literary contribution and heritage of lofty giants and luminaries such as Dickens and George Eliot, among others, postulating to my students how these were literary beacons to the world and were certainly behind my inspiration to study literature at university.

"I know this may not make sense to you folks, but it was because of Dickens, George Eliot, Daniel Defoe, and Wilkie Collins, among others, that I was able to board a plane from Zimbabwe to come here to England to teach you."

"How do you mean, sir?"

"Well, I studied English, didn't I?" I remarked with a mischievous grin. "So, take it this way: if I hadn't studied English at university, I wouldn't be here, teaching English in England, would I?"

"Oh yes, dummy; we get it now, Sir," mused some of them, laughing at my long-winded analogy between Dickens and my getting on a plane to England as an economic migrant.

My love for metaphors was legendary amongst my students. "We know the man loves metaphors," they would often remark, in a tongue-in-cheek reference to myself, as I used to enjoy calling out in my classrooms, bawling at the top of my voice, depersonalizing myself, with the rallying call, "The man is still waiting for silence, before he can proceed." This often fascinated the students who would then innocently remark, "Sir, why do you call yourself "the man?"

"Mum is the word, Angelica!"

"Mum is the word, but my mum is not here sir; are you calling my mum a word, when she's home, sir? I'm going to tell. I'll get you done for insulting my mum, Sir."

"It's a metaphor for you to be quiet, Angelica! Don't you know the man loves metaphors," shouted Kristian, one of the smarty pants lads.

"Okay Kristian, thanks, but you need to play your own drum," I remarked, at which point Jaiden started persistently tapping on his desk with his palms.

"Jaiden, will you stop. Do you hear me?"

"But you just said we can play our own drums a few minutes ago, Sir," crafty Jaiden tried to feign innocence.

"It's a metaphor, which meant, don't get involved in other people's business. Now will you allow the man to do some teaching please?"

Then there was that one afternoon, period 5, last lesson of the day, with a Year 8 English group. I found myself remarking in exasperation at the rampant silliness that day, "...to put things in perspective, my son Brooklyn is twelve, just like you lot, and I have no qualms about telling him off, just like I do with you all, when you step out of line..."

"Is he good looking?" shouted Jenny, one of the naughty girls, amid raucous laughter from the class. I must admit, I initially struggled to keep a straight face, and even though miffed, I lost my composure and bawled into laughter at this cheekiness.

"See, Jenny, you've made Sir to laugh," quipped Tom. As my laughter subsided, and I finally managed to compose myself, I shot back at the errant girl, "Behave yourself, Jenny, will you?"

These were just some of the many exchanges I had with my students, the young minds I taught, who went on to excel in later life. And for that, I am immensely proud to have contributed in nation-building and manpower development, nurturing these youngsters.

CHAPTER 17

Great Hall Swan Song Tribute

Valediction Forbid Mourning

When I eventually left teaching, I bowed down on a high, with honor and humility. I remember vividly delivering my valedictory speech in the school's great hall before an audience packed to the rafters. Clearing my throat, it dawned on me, I had anticipated this moment, the crowning moment of a career well served. I stepped to the podium and took the microphone, fired up now with my well-rehearsed speech: "It's been a life well lived, nurturing these youngsters and their nascent dreams. For those years I got a thank you card, an appreciation email, a subject-specific present, it's meant a lot to me. Equally, for each and every student who's done very well, kudos to you folks! You are my true heroes. You daily validate my passion on why I entered into teaching, to make a positive difference in young children's lives. As you go out into the world and beyond, be that inspirational role model. I have always been accountable to you, beholden to you as my constituency, not a lesson observation, school league tables, or systemic racism which comes out to prejudge and condemn me to oblivion."

I paused after this lengthy introduction, like they do at election rallies, waiting for the party faithful to give that rapturous, rousing applause, but I'm not sure I heard that stirring applause to my retirement eulogy. I had an embarrassing wait, in anticipation; still the adulation and standing ovation did not materialize. Ah well...so much for gratitude and acknowledgment to me for putting in all those years of service.

I am still trying to get my head around this; I can't work this shit out. Today was meant to be key, as it marked the onset of my retirement. Funny how I didn't receive any farewell presents. Not only that, fancy, not even getting bravos for one who has done so much for Brackley and the wider community. Are people not that grateful enough for my years of loyal service at Brackley School? Perhaps now is the time to take stock of my life, reevaluate my goals, and see which other interests I can pursue, post-retirement. It's been a phenomenal journey teaching. So long, fellas.

I can feel my eyes heavy with sleep now; I am getting drowsy again. Perhaps I need to retire to bed, but I can also feel the pounding in my head, that persistent throbbing pain. Have you ever felt pain like a drilling machine, drilling into your brain, whilst you are awake? That's what I get with these migraines. I knew it; it's those goddamn awful tablets they are constantly pumping into us. Bill said it the other day, so it's not me alone, in case you go blaming me again, "There he starts on us." I know I'm an easy target, aren't I? It's always my fault when things kick off in this place. But you know what? Please yourself, I couldn't care any less now. We've been through this before, many times, and you always want to win, and have the last word, always.

Let me take a breather, a siesta may well do me some good. My eyelids are drooping, becoming heavy with sleep. I see people; they are coming after me, but it was never my idea. I don't see how I'm culpable for all these accusations. All I ever did was to love these women, unreservedly for that matter, but what do I get? A kick in my bollocks!

Okay, fellas, won't be long; allow me to recuperate. So long, folks. One thing though, I am disappointed, I haven't got the rousing staff send-off I so rightly deserve. Do you know how hard that is to stomach? For someone who has been part of the school for so long a time? Through those years of drought and hunger, in special measures, out of special measures, when there was massive staff exodus, and I stayed put. Why did I hang around? Because I'm a sucker for loyalty, aren't I?

After all those years of loyal service, giving it your all, and you don't get an acknowledgment from your professional colleagues. It's more like a kick in the teeth for me. Aaah well, they are calling me now; I can hear their voices getting louder. Get away from me! Give me a break, please. I can't stand those tablets. Why don't you take them yourself? No more physical restraint, I say, no more physical restraint, do you hear me! I will be a good lad, I promise, I will be a good lad.

CHAPTER 18

Ides of March
Coming Clean

I saw Zet sitting in what appeared to be a quiet corner of Little Bury's Restaurant and headed straight towards her, oblivious of the seismic changes which were about to come into my life. I politely waved the waiter away. Whatever it was, judging from the urgency in Zet's voice over the phone, had sapped whatever appetite I had, even though I had always enjoyed Little Bury's succulent meals.

"It had to be a neutral venue because I have to come clean with you, Kundai," Zet said, motioning me to the settee opposite her. She certainly looked less than her usual perky self.

It had been a disturbing call, received early that morning from Zet, in which she sounded intense, insisting, "Let's meet at the Little Bury's. 4 pm on the dot," she had remonstrated. "I have something urgent to share with you."

"So, what is it Zet?" I enquired. "Can you spare me the melodramatics, please?'

"I'm afraid it's not good, Kundai," said Zet, speaking softly. "I want out of our relationship," she blurted out.

"What!" I almost dropped out of my chair. "What are you on about Zet? Where is this coming from? You call me this morning, sounding all distraught, and now this? What's been happening? Enlighten me, please," I entreated her.

"I am leaving for Scotland over this weekend. I have done something terrible to you, Kundai. You have to forgive me," went on Zet, her voice now tremulous.

I was still none the wiser, completely failing to make sense of Zet's outbursts.

I pulled myself together so I could get clarity and get to the bottom of this theatre. "Why don't you calm down, Zet, and really tell me what's going on? For heaven's sake, you're not making sense, Zet. Look at yourself; get a grip," I remarked.

"I'm sorry, Kundai, I'm really sorry. You have to find it in your heart to forgive me for what I've done to you." It was at that point that my heart skipped at hearing that clichéd statement. The last time I had heard it from Kay, a few years back, things didn't end well.

You have to find it within your heart, and forgive me for what I have done, Kundai, was a chilling text message I had once received from Kay, one late Friday afternoon, when we'd just broke from school for our two weeks Christmas break. At the time I received Kay's message, I was on the train from London, buoyed after having done my maiden academic conference presentation at Royal Holloway University, clad in my Obama tee shirt. "I am at the airport with the children on our way to Zimbabwe. Sorry I didn't tell you beforehand, but I just needed some break from you, England, and all the shit in our marriage." Just like that, that was it, in one fell swoop Kay had made an all-important decision to go away for two weeks with the kids without even having the courtesy to inform me! And to add insult to injury, during those two weeks she was in Zimbabwe with the children, they did not even visit Mbuya Mafirakureva, my aged mother, so she could dote and spend some time with her grandchildren, something Kay knew Mother would have immensely enjoyed. But then Kay was a sadist par excellence; exacting pain on people certainly gave her the kicks and something to live for.

I was gutted by Kay's unfeeling and unreasonable actions over this callous, selfish decision of hers, and during her absence I left the house in a huff and went on to stay with Zet for a few weeks. But then, *frailty, thy name is children*, I started to miss my children and I moved back into the matrimonial house, much to Kay's delight, as she used to relentlessly taunt me each time, we had an argument. "Look, Kundai, we shouldn't even be arguing; you'd left the house and came back. Why did you come back? No one wants you here, anyway," Kay would rub it in with sadistic glee. She certainly had a sharp tongue.

And now here was a replay of those words from my own Zet. *I have to find it in my heart to forgive her. What is it with these women? They all tend to parrot the same language, sugar coating it before they land the terminal blow on a man. Are they born from the same womb?* I pondered these contradictions to myself.

Looking up, I saw Zet staring at me with an air of feigned pity on her face, which was worse for me, as I can't stand pity. And then she fired the first salvo, "I am taking Edmund with me. I know how much you adore him, and have treated him as your own..."

Treated Edmund as my own? What was Zettie up to? "What are you up to, Zettie?" I enquired again. I never called her Zettie unless I was unhappy with her, and she knew it. Perhaps that must have been the signal she wanted to stop her theatrics that wretched evening.

And then she twisted the knife in my back with her next words. She surely saved the worst news for the last. "The DNA test results came yesterday morning," she said, pushing a brown envelope towards me.

"What DNA results?" I shouted at her now, having lost all my composure.

"Well, if you let me finish first, without constantly interrupting me, then I can get to the bottom of this," remarked Zet.

"Go on then," I urged, as if the first tip of the knife wasn't piercing enough.

Her next statement jacked the knife further into my back, "I cheated on you with your kid brother, Kian, that summer holiday at your Vumba homestead. Those late-night evenings we stayed up for lager, indulging ourselves in weed, as you went to bed early, that's when the deed occurred."

I didn't interrupt her this time, as my befuddled brain tried to process this jaw-dropping avalanche of information on my life.

"I was never really 100 percent certain Edmund was yours but seeing so much how you doted on him all those evenings, helping out with homework, the innumerable school runs, your excellent dad/son rapport with him, I couldn't bear shattering your blissful life. But you have to understand it's been a difficult many years living with repressed guilt, and today I feel free, and we both can be able to get on with our lives now," Zet opined. "But I'm afraid you won't be able to see Edmund again, as we don't want instability and confusion in the poor boy's life. It's for everyone's good, and you have to understand."

"What do you mean 'we?' You and who when you've just jettisoned me out of your life?" I enquired.

"I mean my new partner, Kian, your brother and I won't have it. I know this may be hard for you, Kundai, but in time you shall get over it. I have been secretly having an affair with Kian and was instrumental in arranging his visa to immigrate to Glasgow Scotland, which will be our new home."

My eyes may as well have popped out of their sockets with this bullshit stuff emitting from Zet's mouth. *Kian, my own blood! Kian, my brother and confidante of many years! How could it be?* All this didn't make sense to me, for I still remembered vividly, the excitement we both felt when Kian got his UK work visa, purportedly to start on a new job in Glasgow, Scotland. Zet and I had both driven to Birmingham International Airport to pick up Kian and it had all been smiles and excitement as Kian emerged from the airport arrivals section, grinning from ear to ear.

"*Makadii Gumbi*; how are you *Samusha*?" I remember asking him triumphantly, as I hugged and back slapped him in jovial spirits. "*Mwapinda Gumbi;* you've made it bro haa." And we all chuckled in our mirth, gaiety, and happiness, with Zet joining in, as well. We were a happy family then, as we chugged down in Zet's Aston Martin along the M40 highway, careering through the West Midlands, Warwickshire County landscape, Shakespeare's birthplace. In no time, the journey to our Milton Keynes home was barely over. It was testament to the joyous nature of the event. We hardly felt the unusually long drive from Birmingham to Milton Keynes. Then, Kian went on to stay with us for over a fortnight, as he was not due to start on his job until the beginning of the month. All this time, I was totally oblivious there could have been anything going on between Zet and Kian. How could I, with the abundance of happiness and merrymaking in the Mafirakureva household? Even when Zet volunteered to drive Kian to Glasgow, I didn't see anything amiss. "Are you sure of that undertaking Zet? It's a huge ask, a seven-hour drive, why not let him take a one-hour flight from London Luton Airport instead?" I advised. "Mind you, I won't be able to join you on this marathon trip, even if you insist, as that's too much driving for me. Besides, I have other commitments this weekend."

Zet had laughed me off, dismissing my disdain of long-distance driving. "No worries, Kuu, it's all on me. I'm happy to do it. Kian is family anyway, isn't he? Family comes first." *She was right in a way,* I quietly rationalised within myself. "What a legend you are Zet, thanks." And that had been it. Zet had braved the seven-hour trip to Scotland with Kian.

"Kundai, are you with me?" Zet jolted me out of my reverie.

I couldn't speak; I couldn't answer her then, it was all too much for me. I kept staring in an abysmal vacant space, all zonked out, as if I was high on some intoxicating substance.

"How do you feel? I'm just checking you're all right. There's no need to be unreasonable, Kuu. After all we can…"

"How do I feel? I want to say fuck you, how about that?" I continued, "You come here to finish with me, and you expect the lovey dovey, oh let's be friends bullshit? Not with me, I'm afraid. No pretense, it doesn't work. It won't stick, Zet! Spare me all those corny platitudes, I've heard them before."

For a moment, she appeared disconcerted, caught off guard, as she nibbled her lower lip like she was thinking, walking through every scenario in her head. I knew I had got her where I wanted, but then she surprised me by pulling another shocker out of her bag.

Looking back, I would have come to terms and forgiven Zet for her treachery, had she not uttered the next words: "Yes, I've enjoyed a clandestine relationship with Kian all these years. I couldn't stand it, all the lying, stealth and sneaking around, even though it gave me the kicks. I hope you won't start banging on about morality, given how you cheated on your first wife with me over the years. It's a fact of life; relationships fail at some point. Accept it and move on. In time you will hear from my solicitors, but I don't anticipate any hiccups as we were not legally married. Accept it, Kundai, and move on." With that, she stood up, hugged me, and walked out of my life for good.

Just like that, she was gone, and by some sad coincidence, Bill Withers' *Ain't No Sunshine When She's Gone*, started playing softly from the Little Bury's music speakers. At that moment, I felt like the world was conspiring against me. Cursing under my breath, I threw the glass ash tray next to me against the wall in front of me, missing the surprised waiter by a whisker, after which I mumbled my half-hearted apologies, "Sorry mate, I'm having a bad day."

As Zettie walked out of my life, I couldn't help but marvel at how she had spectacularly outfoxed and played me, without the slightest hint of pre-warning whatsoever. How did I miss it, the deception? I mean, how do you do that, living with a man all those years, professing your undying love and loyalty, but meanwhile, you're conducting a clandestine relationship?

She is brilliant! I started laughing hysterically, clapping my hands in applause to her sheer brilliance. I couldn't help but muse to myself, so *Zettie had secretly facilitated for Kian's visa while giving me those kisses? She was now off to Scotland, for a new life with Kian and my second son?* It suddenly dawned on me, *I've lost three important people in my life, a partner Zettie, a son Edmund, a brother Kian.* I am not sure whether Zettie's betrayal was the beginning of the end for me, the onset of my downward spiral into depression. I knew I had had a wonderful relationship with Edmund, and it broke my heart to realise, in a cruel fashion, he was not my biological child.

CHAPTER 19

Jacinda

I met Jacinda on an online dating website. It must have been after the Zettie falling out. What especially drew me to Jas was the uncanny coincidence that she hailed from Zimbabwe and was actually living in Zimbabwe when we started our online romance. I mean, what are the odds? You go on Tinder and, bang, the first woman you hook up with happens to be your fellow citizen, and you are in another random part of the world. The coincidence was staggering for me and I took it as a sure signal she would be the one to heal the wounds of my egregious split from Zet. More so, the allure of the name Jacinda, which prompted my interest into checking her online dating profile in the first place, derived from my enamour of New Zealand Prime Minister, sultry Jacinda Arden, my celebrity crush.

We chatted a lot on WhatsApp, did Skype calls and Zoom, then exactly eight months after our first online chat, I flew to Zimbabwe to meet up with Jas. I wasn't disappointed with what I saw of Jas. Given our daily online liaisons, we felt over-familiar with each other during my two weeks stay in Zimbabwe, and by the end of the visit I had proposed to Jas and she acquiesced to be my wife.

There were hurdles ahead, not least the pitfalls of a long-distance relationship, and the visa process, in itself an arduous journey, to enable Jas to come and live with me in England. My daughter Alexis, now a successful human rights lawyer working between London and Amsterdam, gave me a friendly warning to not jump into another relationship, "So soon again Daddy?"

But I rudely brushed her aside. "For fuck sake, Alexis, give me a break, is this to do with your mother again? Tell you what, when I need your relationship advice, I will make an appointment with your PA, but now is not the time, thank you," I shooshed her away.

In happier days, before the Zet debacle, Kian used to say of me, I was too headstrong when it came to women, and once, I'd set my mind on a woman, none would dissuade me. Even if it was a foolhardy choice, I was not for turning. A couple of times, Kian had admonished me, "Be careful, don't conflate your lust for women as love. Get your head straight first, before committing." Maybe he was right, I don't know. *Maybe, I'm like Shakespeare's tragic hero, with a regrettable flaw*, I mused to myself.

Jas worked in a commercial bank in Zimbabwe as a human resources executive, and she told me she was an only child. Not much family to talk of. Both her parents had tragically died in a car accident in which she was the only survivor, and miraculously emerged unscathed when she was a teenage girl; the local vicar in her neighbourhood had raised her as his own.

Perhaps I was either blinded or too gullible. I did not see any red flags in this, "*I am an only child' story*" and thus, did not think of checking it out. Could it not have been inconceivable, Jas was trying to deliberately rewrite her personal history and conveniently obliterate her past? I didn't think of this wisdom at the time. I was in love. I can be such a hopeless romantic.

Applying for a UK spouse visa was a painstaking invasive process which entailed putting together a voluminous paper trail of evidence supported by proof of relationship, adequate accommodation, bank statements, and meeting a minimum £18,600 annual income threshold to satisfy the UK home office before they could issue out a spouse settlement visa. As if that weren't a deterrent enough, the application fee and other attendant costs were outrageously astronomical, with no cast iron guarantee of landing the visa after forking out a fortune and spending onerous time gathering the tedious supporting paperwork.

Thus, it took two refusals and an immigration tribunal court appearance before Jas was awarded her spouse visa enabling her to join me in England. On the day she picked up her passport at the British Consular in Harare, with the vignette visa sticker affixed, she noticed and alerted me the accompanying letter with her passport made it clear, the visa was only for two-and-a-half years, after which we would have to reapply for a further two-and-a-half years, once the current visa was about to lapse, and it would be a rerun of the first application, with all the finances again.

There's certainly no respite for the wicked!

Jas flew to England a week after picking up her passport and I drove to Heathrow Terminal 5 to pick her up. Part of me felt a sense of de ja vu as I reflected, thinking of March 2002 when pregnant Kay had been waiting to pick me up also at Heathrow. I felt like the wheel had come full circle now, that I was also picking up my own woman in a similar fashion. *Hopefully, there would be no drama this time*, I whispered within myself as I hugged Jas.

Jas had no teething problems acclimatising to life in England, as in no time, she got a job with the local Halifax Bank as a customer service representative. I wasn't much surprised with this, as Jas had the gift of the gab and oozed confidence within her persona. She was the sort of person who could sell ice to the Eskimos, and they would sure buy it without batting an eye.

Initially, things seemed to be flowing well in our mundane lives. The only problem though, was that both my children, Alexis and Brooklyn, made it clear they didn't want to accept Jas in their lives, not that she gave a hoot herself. "Life goes on, Kundai; you can't expect to be loved by everyone. Anyway, I'm not their biological mother, I get, it," Jas said.

There were moments when we could go out a lot, sometimes to the West End theatre in London, or an evening out for a quiet drink to the local pubs. It was then I could see flashes of a Jas who loved her drink a tad too much and became quite loquacious once she'd had one too many. But I didn't pay much attention to it. I thought, *okay, we all love our drink once in a while, don't we? There's no harm in indulging our guilty pleasures.*

However, Jas also had some eccentricities in her mundane life.

There were moments I could catch her face in a perpetual vacant stare, and upon asking her, "Is everything all right, honey?" she would always allay my fears. Or I noticed, on occasions, she would spend excessively long periods of time in the bathroom. I would end up checking on her, all very weird. Then there was also what appeared to be the delirious talking in her sleep, the profuse sweating upon walking up. "Don't you think you ought to see a shrink for your talking and delirium at night, love?" I gingerly broached the subject to her one evening.

"I've told you before, there's nothing wrong with me. Why do you keep asking me the same questions over and over? I'm not daft!" That was the very first time I noticed Jas's flaming temper and she snapped at me here. I was taken aback and recoiled into my inner shell as I didn't want any conflict.

I tried to rationalise her weird, erratic behaviour and ascribed it to childhood trauma caused by the tragic car accident which had robbed her of her parents and a normal childhood. In retrospect, marriage sometimes feels like servitude, where one party has to put up with the antics of an odious party, for fear of unintended consequences or rejection. And I was increasingly beginning to feel more like this. I think I was trapped in a vicious cycle of guilt, self-recrimination, especially given that my previous relationships had all failed. I couldn't bear the social opprobrium and censure of my relationship with Jas failing, as well, so I started making up excuses for her, for the drinking, which started to rear its ugly head every now and then; for the unexplained curtness to me, which started to gradually increase.

Once I suggested, "Why don't we try for a baby?" and it was like I had suggested having her head chopped off on a guillotine. "What for?" she remarked incredulously. "Why do you need more children, when you already have them?" Her voice was almost shrill in reply.

"Ah, I thought it would be nice for us to have a little Kundai and mini-Jas."

"Not remotely interested!" she shot me down at once. "You already have children from your previous relationships, so it's no from me." Jas went on, "I know I don't have biological children myself, but have you heard me whining? No, and in any case, it's not like you are getting any younger, Kundai. You are 47 now, and you tell me you still want to have kids? Have you actually thought this through? And do you realise you need over £100k to look after a child, up until they go through university? Not for me, not in my name, I'm afraid." And with that she brusquely left the room for upstairs, leaving me flabbergasted.

When she eventually joined me later that evening in bed, her breath was foul and reeking of alcohol and cigarettes; the latter surprised me as I didn't know she smoked. I was too timid to ask the next morning, as I didn't want to be subjected to another humiliating lecture and dressing down.

I must admit, the weeks following the baby talk incident, my daughter's words of pre-warning for me to take time before jumping into a relationship with Jas crossed my mind, and I quickly brushed them aside. I was too embarrassed to acknowledge to myself that I was approaching a more familiar pattern of relationship breakdown like in the past. *In any case, I'm imagining all this; it's in my head,* I reassured myself. *Jas is a lovely woman, and I want this marriage to work.* I reaffirmed this mantra within myself. Never underestimate the power of self-delusion.

And then I discovered Jas' secret in the bathroom!

Unbeknown to me, Jas was on anti-retroviral therapy taking HIV tablets secretly, and I only discovered this accidentally from her diary. And upon snooping around in the house, I saw how she used to hide her stash of anti-retroviral therapy tablets in a false case opening in our bathroom cabinet. I was stunned! I felt like I had been pummelled by a sledgehammer and then shoved under a tonne of bricks. *Frailty, thy name is woman…*I said to myself slouching down on the floor, as I started sobbing, my head drooping in my shoulders. I will never forget the feeling of emptiness that engulfed me. I felt sick in the pit of my stomach with this discovery.

Amidst all this turmoil, I couldn't help but reflect, *was this my mea culpa, these incessant mishaps with women? Why doesn't there seem to be a let up?*

That evening, Jas returned from work to see me still waiting up for her. She could tell from my stony face that something was up, and it must be something quite big and serious. I was still reeling from my discovery, trying to come to terms with it, but equally, I realised I had to be kind and sensitive how I broached the subject of my discovery to Jas. I mean, tell me, how do you confront your wife and say, *I realise you are taking HIV medication secretly, why have you been hiding it from me?* It's not that easy, is it?

Clearing my throat and choosing my words carefully, I made my opening pitch, "Ah, I think we need to talk, sweetie."

"What is it about?" replied Jas. "Can't it wait until tomorrow? I'm having a bad day, unless it's something cheery."

It didn't look like I was going to get anywhere, but the thought of sleeping over it was not something I was prepared to stomach, so this thought emboldened me to blurt my thoughts out, "I'm afraid I know about your secret, aaah, the bathroom secret…" I stammered. I couldn't bear to come clean about having read her private diary.

Jas looked right through me for a while without speaking, and after an awkward silence of what seemed eternity, she said softly, "I feel free today. In a way I'm relieved you now know the truth."

I responded, "But why the deception, Jas? Why couldn't you come clean with me in the first place? It's not like we are talking of a minor illness here. I am not judgemental, far from it, but you owe me the truth; that is all I ask for." My voice was now quivering with emotion as I spoke.

Jas held both my hands then she remarked, "It was equally difficult for me to tell you about this, Kundai. I agonised over telling you the truth, but then as my viral load is undetectable, I reckoned, there was no need to tell. I know I was selfish, honey, but I didn't want to lose you, after all the tragedies in my life. You're the only friend I have. As my HIV is undetectable, I gambled by not telling you. We could still have our normal life," she went on, but this was getting too much for me.

"Is that why you were not keen to get pregnant?" I shot back. "Ahm, I see it now, you had it all planned, didn't you?"

"Not at all," she denied, then she started sobbing. "Please forgive me, Kundai. Are we still cool?" she asked amid her tears, boring her eyes into me again, like she was trying to put me under a captivating spell.

"I don't know Jas," I whispered hoarsely, "I really need some time to process all this. You have to understand this is earth shattering news for me. It's not so much the HIV stigma for me, but your wilful, conscious decision to withhold the truth from me."

Knowing about Jas's HIV and how she'd concealed it from me hit me very hard, perhaps much harder than I had anticipated. I became increasingly paranoid about what else she was hiding from me, if she can have the bravado to be that deceptive for the three years, we'd been together? Jas was no fool either. Upon realizing she'd been found out, our relationship increasingly took a sharp knocking, which saw a reincarnation of the squabbling of yesteryear that I thought had gone away with the Kay divorce. First, it was the drinking, which I noticed started to get out of hand. I always knew Jas liked her drink, but previously she had always managed to be a moderate drinker, with some over the top drinking, here and there. And now, when I tried to query the drinking, that's what ignited the verbal rows and onslaughts.

Unbeknown to me at the time, Jacinda started playing the domestic violence card, on the behest of secret legal advice she was getting from a chat show hostess, cum Zimbabwean lawyer, Rufaro Makoni, who was advising her. Building a case of sustained violence charges against me as the perpetrator would help secure her legal stay in England. We were still on the first of her 2-and-a-half year spouse visa route, which needed to be renewed at the end of this time frame. And this was drawing near in about six months' time.

Once, I came home early from work on Jas's off day. She must have been oblivious of my presence in the house, as I could hear snippets of a Skype call, she was having with someone on the other end. As her volume was quite loud, I managed to pick up the gist of what the person on the other end was saying.

"So, do I have a chance?"

"To secure your legal status here, we…inaudible muffle…we…we have to build a credible case that your husband has been physically violent towards you. Seeing as you don't have children, that's your only meal ticket to enable you to remain legal…Then we can always ratchet up pressure and ramp in the women domestic violence advocates, lobby groups to give gravitas to your case."

I didn't wait to hear anymore; what I'd heard was enough to tip me over the edge. Without warning I barged into the living room where Jas was having her Skype call, and lo and behold, I noticed notorious Zimbabwe immigration lawyer, nasty Rufaro, as the person on the other end of the Skype call. Momentarily stunned by my abrupt entrance, both women froze in mid-conversation and Jas angrily pressed the red phone icon on her MacBook, instantly terminating her call.

"Aaaah, I see, so is this what you are now planning against me Jas?" She could only look at me as if she were a little kid, caught with her fingers in the cookie jar. "Answer me, Jas, don't be cowardly. I deserve a conversation with you. You can't blank me out just like that!"

Somewhat finding her voice with an ugly tone in it, she vehemently retorted, "I have nothing to discuss with you, Kundai. How dare you disrupt a private phone conversation. Anyway, it's not what you think." And with that, she grabbed her laptop and stormed out of the living room leaving me more dazed and confused. Sadly, that had increasingly become the norm in our marriage, living as antagonistic opponents. In hindsight, this odd Skype call with crooked Zim lawyer Rufaro should have forewarned me that the end was nigh with Jas, but perhaps the hopeless romantic that I am refused to countenance this.

Inwardly, I rued the day I had unwittingly introduced Jas to this unscrupulous immigration lawyer through sharing with Jas how Rufaro had managed to extricate my maternal Uncle Sekuru Kumire from getting into detention over a litany of immigration offences.

"You see *muzukuru*, Rufaro is a top-notch immigration lawyer. She arranged this fake Portugal passport for me, and as an EU citizen under my freedom of movement rights, I am able to work in this country," Sekuru would brag to me, waving away my misgivings.

"But Khule, isn't that risky for you? Can you imagine what you stand to lose in the event you're found out?"

"But everything is risky in life, whichever way you look at it. So instead of moping in misery, feeling sorry for myself, I would rather get busy living, rather than dying."

That was vintage Uncle Kumire, with his usual bluff, bluster and bravado optimism.

And so, it came to pass, when sekuru Kumire fell out with his live-in wife, she shopped him to the Home Office that he didn't have papers, which allowed him right of residency and permission to work in England. The UK Border Force police immigration unit was heavy handed in their response to Sekuru's predicament, and they threw him in Belmarsh Prison Immigration and Asylum Detention Centre.

"Good old Rufaro Makoni, my astute lawyer saved the day for me," Sekuru was later to recount to me, amid guffaws of laughter at his near- miss misfortune which would have landed him a custodial sentence for possession of a fraudulent passport. Notwithstanding Sekuru's blasé attitude, I didn't regard it as funny, as he missed a prison sentence by a whisker. "Well, the thing is, Rufaro pulled out a couple of rabbits from her proverbial legal bag of tricks, not least Article 8, The EU Human Rights Act, the right to family, which meant I couldn't be deported to Zimbabwe on account of my two sons with my ex, even though we'd been cohabiting, and not legally married," Uncle said.

"What about your passport fraud, Khule?" I countered. "Does that not count as identity fraud? Surely, the old Bailey would have got you on that one."

"Aaaah, you see, not unless you have the best legal brains as Rufaro. The thing is, she cooked up a convincing story which she made me to rehearse to the immigration and asylum tribunal judge, who seemed to have fallen for my contrition yarn, hook, line and sinker."

"I'm sorry, Your Honor, I was made to believe I was eligible for an EU passport and rightly paid for its acquisition through what

I deemed were legitimate channels. However, I am genuinely remorseful at my poor judgement. In retrospect, I can appreciate I was duped and taken advantage of. I apologize unreservedly for my gross error of judgement."

"Really, Khule, and just like that, the judge fell for it?"

"Oh yes! He did. Just like that, as you say. I got away with a suspended custodial sentence and a strong warning never to flout immigration laws again. But to be honest, who cares about a criminal record when now I can get to stay in England legally, and get to see my two boys. Everyone wins, end of story."

And now I painfully realised, sharing Sekuru's anecdotal immigration shenanigans had inadvertently introduced Jas to wily Rufaro Makoni, the insidious Zimbabwe immigration lawyer, whose influence was about to exacerbate my marital woes.

Following her dark secret's expose, I had numerous rows with Jacinda, which unfortunately were mostly played out on social media on her part, and in some cases live streamed on Facebook, Twitter, and YouTube, as Jas had developed into a narcissistic attention seeker. In one instance, after a falling out, I was embarrassed when family members alerted me to a Facebook post which was doing the rounds and had gone viral, in which, lo and behold, I saw my very own Jas staring at me from the computer screen, tearful and pouring her heart out with our domestic titbits' dirty linen, accusing me of orchestrating verbal violence against her.

This tipped me over the edge, too, and I confronted her head on, "What are you on about, Jas, embarrassing me like this on social media?" I charged. "Are you out of your fucking mind?" I bellowed.

"Well, I could ask the same of you," countered Jas. "Since your so-called expose, you've become increasingly mean and emotionally unavailable to me. You don't touch me anymore, not even make love to me," she retorted.

"What do you mean?" I looked at her bewildered. "Oh, so I'm supposed to be lovey dovey with you when you lied to me big time? We haven't even discussed about having medical tests; at least I need those for my own peace of mind," I was almost shouting at her. "And now you're drinking like a fish," I said, sneering at her.

"Social media is therapeutic to me," remarked Jas. "It's my way of dealing with our issues," she went on.

"Oh, I see, what a clever way of dealing with private issues, making oneself an idiot on a public forum!" I countered. "Do you even think of the implications on my job if you post such brazen accusations online?" I carried on, "And just so you know, the internet has a long memory; it doesn't forget. Does it not even worry you, the indelible digital footprints you are leaving behind with all this?" I charged at her.

"It's always your job, isn't it?" retorted Jas. "Everything has to revolve around that sordid job. Well sod it!" Jas said, giving me the two-finger salute.

Inwardly, I hated these diatribes; it was underhanded and nasty, the sort of life I thought I had parked in the Kay era, but there you are. Looks like the wheel had come full circle for me, again!

"You know, Jas," I said, soothingly, trying to be the bigger person, "You have really wronged me by posting a Facebook video, baring our privacy to the outside world. There's really no need for this kind of behaviour. I hope it won't happen again." But I may as well have spoken too soon. In subsequent months, Jas seemed to have taken an affinity for broadcasting our minutiae private details of our life on various online platforms.

It was at that point that I requested we both seek medical counselling and Jas blatantly refused to even consider it, "Medical counselling, what for? That's preposterous." She charged, "If you think you need it, then you can go by yourself."

Perhaps it was also around this tetchy time that I started to lose interest in life and began to withdraw into myself more and more. I vividly remember Sue Velma, my other surrogate mother as I called her, the Librarian at The Brackley School, fussing over me, overly concerned for my welfare as she noticed I had become increasingly unkempt and scruffy at school at times missing school for days on end yet forgetting to inform the school hierarchy in line with the laid down absenteeism protocols for staff. Good old Sue had always looked out after me well at Brackley and was ever so protective of me right from my early days of my arrival at the school. Her constant entreaties to my welfare enquiring whether everything was all right at home, may just have signalled to her and the outside world my personal and gradual descent into a hell-hole dark place. Once she repeatedly asked after me and I brusquely brushed her aside; "I'm just trying to help, remember Kundai, anytime you need to talk, The Vicar will always be there for you," she prodded one morning, when I had been late to school again, and came in with uncombed hair and my necktie missing. "Oh, it's nothing Sue, believe me, everything is hunky dory," I dismissed her though inwardly my turmoil with my personal issues had just about reached tipping point. Once, another colleague Dan accused me of reeking alcohol stench at break-time mid-morning, but I dismissed him as mistaken. "Man, you're mistaken, me reeking of alcohol so early on in the morning, mid-week for that matter. Are you sure your sense of smell is not failing you? You do realise loss of smell is one sure sign of Covid Dan? You may well need to go and get tested Dan seriously." I rudely fobbed Dan off, but I doubt he fell for it as he's always been an astute fella and good friend. Was I becoming delusional and in denial of my own need for help?

I couldn't confide in my daughter Alexis, because I knew she blamed me for the split with her mother. Perhaps I had a chance for an audience with Brooklyn. Edmund was out of reach, since Zet had taken him to Scotland, together with Kian. Inwardly, I branded myself a failure. Three relationships all seemed to have come to nought, then there were those lost years, those years of drought and hunger when I couldn't see my children, as Kay dragged me through the family court, obstructing contact, maligning my integrity with those malicious unsavoury untruths about my character. Surely, there has to be some justice of some sort in this wretched world. I was beginning to feel sorry for myself and I hated this self-pitying exercise.

In retrospect, the whole domestic abuse charade, online documenting of our lives now appears a well-choreographed plan to ensure Jas would secure her papers or legal status in the country. It meant the case generated high profile publicity, which in turn served Jacinda's calculating mind well. Mind boggling how you live with a person under the same roof, only to later realise, you didn't actually know anything about them. Who would have thought Jas was such a twisted fucker! Given the nature of my job as a public servant at a high-profile high school, I received a flurry of enquiries from journalists wanting my side of the story on allegations of domestic violence against my wife. *"Do you think this is in order, for a man of your stature to be holding a position of trust, yet bash your wife secretly, by night?"* were some of the remarks thrown at me. I increasingly withdrew into myself, stopped taking calls, even from my daughter Alexis, who must have picked up the furore in the local papers and tried to reach out to me.

Brooklyn visited me, but I couldn't really open up on the finer details of what was happening between me and Jas, other than rambling and philosophising, "You know what, son? I'm going through a rough patch like everyone else, but all will be well. Women, that's women for you. One day you'll walk the road I'm walking." I was banging on the table with a clenched fist as I spoke.

I think I may have underestimated the breakdown of my relationship with Jas. Perhaps it was much worse than my other two fallouts with Kay and Zet. It soon turned out, within weeks, the

Jas fiasco catapulted me into an abysmal depression, especially as I ended up having to attend counselling by myself, ironically for the very domestic abuse she accused me of. Day in day out, I was now on the receiving end of tongue lashing from Jas. I am ashamed to say this, but inwardly I started to feel insecure around Jas, and was increasingly scared of her. Then, just when I thought she couldn't debase herself any further, a further blow came for me when Jas went for a bare-all talk chat show with her Zimbabwean cum chat show hostess- immigration lawyer, in which she "revealed" about how she's suffered domestic abuse from me, after I had deliberately infected her with HIV! This interview was flighted both on Rufaro's Facebook chat show and YouTube channel and generated a huge viewership, particularly from the Zimbabwean community within the United Kingdom, as Rufaro had built something of a cult following for herself.

It looked like my world was falling apart.

I couldn't carry on with work and I requested for compassionate leave on medical grounds, which was speedily granted. My school was not too chuffed with the negativity to the school being generated by the headlines in relation to my private life. I had long read somewhere, "When you're in the public domain, and you become the story; that's the time to quit."

Given the nature of the Media course I taught, it meant I was quite well-known within the Brackley community; my Media department interacted a lot with related media stakeholders who, in some cases organised placement for my students. Some of the local scribes were professional colleagues who would come and deliver career enrichment programs to my sixth form classes. In a typical "hoist made by his own petard case," these professional media relations I enjoyed with Brackley community were to incessantly haunt me, especially when Jas escalated her social media exposes of me.

Feeling increasingly overwhelmed, Alexis arranged and actually frog-marched me to a shrink, and I also went for extensive medical tests in order to ascertain my HIV status; I was hugely relieved I had a near miss at not contracting HIV, though the whole thing scarred me permanently. As the doctors explained to me, we were a discordant couple and it was fairly normal that because Jacinda was taking her medication consistently with an undetectable viral load, this ensured I had inadvertently been shielded from contracting the virus, even though we had regular unprotected sex. Upon hearing this, I wished we had both attended counselling because I thought perhaps this would have helped both of us to cope, and possibly save our marriage, but I had to pull myself up. "Get a grip, Kundai," I muttered in low tones under my breath.

Perhaps, witnessing the rapid decline in my persona and self-esteem, Alexis tried to persuade me to ensure that I kick Jas out of our matrimonial home, but I couldn't do it. "I'm sorry I can't do that, Alexis," I remarked to my daughter. "Notwithstanding what's happened, Jas has every right to be here, and in any case, she needs to sort out her legal status in a few months' time, and I'm not exactly going to throw her out, am I?"

"But that's her own funeral, Dad, it's not like she's treated you well, herself. Look at how she's dredged your name in the gutter and sewer, a respected member of the community, this is what it's come to. I'm not having it Dad," Alexis countered, but I stood firm. Whatever my differences with Jas, I wanted to be decent to her to the bitter end. It wasn't love. *Love, what is love?* I'm not sure I believed in that fantasy world anymore. I had given in to this "love and marriage" thing twice, and once with my partner, Zet, but where had it taken me? Nowhere, other than one cul de sac after the other.

Then the drinking went up a notch higher with Jas, which would put her in fits and bouts of uncontrollable rage. She would be a different being who would lash out at me, and sometimes trade physical blows with me. Once, on a Saturday evening, she was on her bender, downing one lager after the other, after which she moved into cocktails. When I raised my objections to this, before I knew it, Jas was livestreaming her drinking session, interspersed with her little complimentary speech on how I was a bully and a control freak, bent on dictating to her how to live her own life. For the first time, I started to seriously think, Jas was losing it; this was now over the top. Acting decisively, I unplugged the router from its socket and went upstairs with it. That unceremoniously ended her embarrassing Facebook livestream, but it also earned me a barrage of insults as I trudged upstairs, the wireless router firmly clasped under my arm. I was now determined that at some point we needed to sit down together and arrange amicably ending our marriage. I had given it my best shot, but it hadn't worked out, again. Previous attempts at restorative dialogue had failed and I reckoned the only way forward now was to both engage the services of mediators to help us get to talk to each other so, we parted on a good note. But that decision was taken out of my hands by the turn out of events in a few days' time.

The last straw came sooner than I expected. It occurred when, one evening, Jas took my car without my knowledge; she was sky high on alcohol and drove to Tescos Supermarket to buy more alcohol. And on challenging this foolhardy behaviour, she descended on me with fist blows like a sledgehammer. That was the Rubicon moment for me. I didn't need any further signal. I phoned the police, and they took her away. Drink driving was not something they took lightly here, especially after they breathalysed her, and she was found to be four times over the permissible legal limit! I chose not to press charges for the physical assault against me because, deep down, I realised Jas was a troubled soul who needed some professional therapy and tender loving care, though it was clear, I was not that person who was able to do that for her.

CHAPTER 20

Confinement

Reconciling with the Past

"Can you please take your tablets? I'm not in the mood today, Kundai," barked one of the carers glaring at me. "Today is your important review day with your psychiatrist," she further shouted at me, waving a cocktail of tablets in my face, much to my annoyance. They are supposed to be carers, aren't they? They all treat us like we're stupid, a piece of shit, but I am lucid and fully compos mentis, though I've managed to evade and fool the system, all these months, after I was forcibly brought here against my will. My children's fault, committing me to an asylum like this. "Oh daddy, it's for your own good," my all-knowing daughter, Alexis had falsely reassured me, but I knew the real reason: They couldn't bear to live with me under the same roof, following my third and acrimonious split with Jacinda, their third stepmother. They resented me, blamed me for the chaos which my life had become accustomed to since I split from their mother. Perhaps, my children had had enough, so they hatched this devious plan with Bucks County Council Social Services to declare me mentally unfit to live by myself.

"It's not safe for him," many evenings I could overhear Alexis speaking in hushed tones downstairs over the phone. "He did it again today, smashed all the dinner plates in the house, plastered the dining room wall with handprints of his faeces. I can't do it. I'm sorry, I know he is my dad. I'm sorry, you have to section him," whined Alexis in her pitiful, annoying voice. "First it was the attempted drowning incident in the bathtub, the long hospital stays, and now this," went on Alexis. What bathtub incident? *What is she on about,* I pondered within myself?

And so, after several weeks of me playing defiant, one sultry evening, reminiscent of *sisi* Nyari of the Edmonton flat fame, I was forcibly jettisoned out of my daughter's opulent manor house, and swiftly checked into Wendover Heights, a 40-residents, semi residential house for loonies like myself, though they tried to couch it under the phrase, "Oh, we are sectioning you for your own good; they'll look after you well here, Daddy." *Look after me well? I haven't seen that yet, the past seven months I've been here.*

These snorty bitches couldn't care less about us, myself and my mate, Bill, but we are smart. Daily, they pump us with heavy doses of these goddam awful tablets. "Give him trazodone, up his olanzapine dose, he is kicking off again," we hear the damn carers barking their mean remarks, but I am always one step ahead of them, I keep the tablets in my mouth, pretend to swallow, and spit them out later, in the privacy of my bathroom, when they are not looking. If bathrooms could tell tales, mine would have a best seller. Whatever happened to the *Shona* cultural values, whereby, we look after our own aged parents and not commit them to old people's prisons conveniently disguised as care homes? Perhaps, as I've often reflected within myself, in my moments of solitude, I should have just gone back to Zimbabwe, following the litany of misfortunes which have come my way. Maybe things would have turned out differently in Zimbabwe. Zimbabwe would have given me a much more grounded woman, who would have stood by me, through thick and thin, not these fly-by-night mercenaries like Jas...

Dear diary, today, is one of those big days. I am expecting a visit from my son, Brooks. I always look forward to Brooks visiting me. At least, he treats me with compassion and respect, unlike his sister, that mean bitch, Alexis. Can you believe, Alexis has only visited me twice in seven months? First, when she dumped me here with the connivance of the police, and secondly, when I passed out because of my protest hunger strike, as I was making a principled stand on being detained here against my will.

I saw them first before they had noticed me, Zeppelin or Dr. Death, as Bill and I called him, the loonies' senior shrink, talking in earnest to my son Brooklyn, who looked bemused. Bill and I called him Dr. Death because there was something ghoulish and unsettling about Zeppelin's physical persona, and his piercing red eyes didn't put him in any good stead either, resting on that perpetually bald head of his. Zeppelin also reminded me of a cross between Dominic Cummings and a wolf, especially those crafty looking eyes. Bill and I are convinced little children would burst into tears, scared stiff, on the horrific sight of Dr. Zeppelin. "Most likely, they will also have perpetual nightmares," I always added with a chuckle. They must have felt my eyes boring on them, for they turned around abruptly and, upon noticing me, Dr. Death went into his all too familiar character, his scripted façade performance, being all super friendly to me. Of course, it was fake. Zeppelin knew it. I knew it, even as he beckoned both Brooklyn and me to one of the private consulting rooms. "Hello, Kundai, lovely to meet you. It's all good here, just routine meeting with both you and your son, Brooklyn."

"Well, why don't we shelve this claptrap, and cut straight to the chase Dr?" I remarked.

Somewhat taken aback, clearing his throat, Zeppelin went into his other alter ego performance, speaking solemnly, addressing my son Brooklyn, "I'm sorry to have to say this Brooklyn, but there is no nicer way of sugar-coating this, but your father is in an advanced state of psychosis. We can't help him; no one can. Medical intervention by way of tablets has reached its course. He is delusional and it can only upset him further to try to take him out of that fantasy world he has created for himself, for so long."

That must have been too much for poor Brooklyn. His voice trembling, he ejaculated, "But that is cruel to Dad, Doctor. Surely you can do something. I mean, that's not my dad I keep looking at each time I come here. Do you wanna know why my sister can't bear coming in? It's the thought of witnessing Dad in a delirious state, spouting hogwash!"

"It's a kind of fantasy bubble," coughed, the resident psychiatrist, before he resumed speaking, "but I can assure you, we have done everything we can do for your father, and as harsh as it sounds, this is where it ends: medical intervention, but…" Zeppelin cleared his throat, his voice quivering, he hesitated to speak.

"But what?" I gleefully interjected.

"There's this new drug, clinical trials, we could put him on." Zeppelin spoke, looking intently into Brooklyn's eyes.

"Really?" I could see Brooks looking incredulous at all this. Must say, I was enjoying it, if I have managed to pull it off even for the learned doctor not to see that I'm faking it, then I must be bloody brilliant! I felt euphoric and elated within myself.

Dr. Death continued speaking, "There is, however, a slim chance your father may be able to slip out of his semi-zombie status. It's possible; it's happened to a tiny fraction of our patients. So, if you're not in favour of clinical, experimental trials, then we defer to natural healing therapy."

It was at that time I couldn't contain my laughter anymore, hearing the learned doctor utter such bullshit to my son. I've heard baloney in my life before, but this was way out of my league. I just couldn't stop laughing; I went into guffaws of uncontrollable laughter, thinking where on earth did, they extract Zeppelin from? Such a charlatan passing off as a psychiatrist doctor, and poor Brooklyn seeming to be confused and on the verge of falling for it.

As I continuously bellowed into my now hysterical laughter,

they all looked at me weirdly again, like I was an object of comedy to them. I waved my arm peremptorily. "Enough! Brooklyn let the good doctor excuse us. Time for a quiet man-to-man chat with Daddy. You can go on with this shit at some point if you are interested. Not now for me. Time to catch up with me, young man. So long, Zeppelin," I sneered at him sarcastically, and he mumbled inaudibly before he left us.

We had an awkward encounter after Dr. Death left us, as Brooklyn tried to take the good doctor's side, "Well, Dad, you really ought to cooperate with the doctors and follow what they say. It's been seven months now, and clearly, you're unwell."

"And so, I need help. Let me spare you the trouble, Brooks, and finish it for you," I sarcastically replied to him, "and before you go on, yes, I'm in denial like Alcoholics Anonymous, aren't I? Anything else, son, or are we done today?" He could see I was fired up and was having none of it that day. Eventually Brooklyn left without both of us having any common ground.

Well, so much for my touted visit from Brooks, such a damp squib after all, as it appears Brooks has closed ranks with his two sisters, in pigeonholing me, a silly old man, who has had a breakdown he doesn't want to accept or come to terms with. "You are in denial, Dad... Take it within your stride. This is not a prison, far from it. We are all doing what we can with the carers here to look after you." Can you believe it, those words coming from Brooks, such betrayal? How can I be insane, a paranoid schizophrenic as they term me, if I can still be able to clearly articulate and document my life, as I have done these past few months?

"And, you know what, I am at peace with myself, Brooklyn," I said it with a flourish of my hand, waving dismissively at him. "Why don't we change the subject?" I said to him. "I've always had a good rapport with you, unlike your two sisters, and I want it to remain that way," I remarked, and so we talked about other things, laughing and reminiscing with my boy, Brooklyn.

And when it came to parting later that evening, I couldn't help but reflect how I deeply loved all my children, even Zettie's illegitimate son, sired with my brother, little Edmund; well, not so little anymore. I long ago came to terms with Zettie's betrayal; it wasn't Edmund's fault, it was no one's fault, not even Kay's fault for the failure of the first marriage. I had loved Kay, wholeheartedly, I think, the mother of my three children, it hadn't worked out, that's a fact of life with relationships. You win some, you lose some, *If Only*, as a classic Rod Stewart ballad goes...Having been close to Kay, all those years, and now knowing what I know now about her, the constant struggle with bipolar disorder which she strove to conceal. I know Kay's heart and understand her words sometimes did not always align with her intentions. Perhaps, in retrospect, there was no need for that acrimony which had punctuated the protracted legal wrangling, as I tried to establish contact with the children. But I forgive Kay now. I am at peace with everyone, the duplicitous Zet and my wicked, backstabbing Judas brother, Kian, who had seen it fit to cuckold me with my partner Zet. Even the vivacious Jacinda and her volatile temper, the drinking, the needless violence, I forgive her also. *Yes, life is beautiful, but we all miss it,* I reflected, as I reached for my cigarette.

Perhaps I should be grateful to have had my safety net, my family support network, particularly Alexis and Brooklyn, and I could also take refuge in my inner groundedness. My mea culpa, the unwitting cathartic involvement with women, meant I have been walking on shifting ground all these years, but I accept it. The wheel has come full circle. The truth hurt, jagged like a dog bite, but there was something liberating in being honest with oneself, confronting my demons head on, as I called it.

I have capacity. How else have I managed to keep my thoughts consistently in my secret diary, and yet the powers that be here, continue to misrepresent my persona? I silently mused to myself. But I so want to go home; these voices are taking over my personal space. How many times do I have to say this to those damn fools, the carers, for them to take me seriously? Perhaps, I will try again through Brooklyn; he may be able to assist me, or better still, I may have to rope in Alexis after all, the genesis of my ordeal.

Anyway, I need to finalize arrangements with Alexis who brought me here, to terminate this whole thing; this sick joke should come to an end now. "Okay, you've made your point Alexis, you win, I give you this, but I have pressing commitments to attend to. I haven't seen my students in ages; they need me, I can hear their voices, I can see them beckoning. Soon, it will be summer, the onset of exam time, and I need to prep my exam classes."

ACKNOWLEDGMENTS

To Priveledge and our son, Brooklyn, Manatha, you are my dream team and I love you forever. Thank you for being incredible.

Special credit goes to famed author, friend, and esteemed colleague, Memory Chirere, for your honest and wise counsel in the early days of writing this book. And to Dr. Watson, Arthur my little brother, thanks for availing me the platform for my voice to be heard. I offer bottomless gratitude to my colleague, writer, and sister, Zukiswa Wanner, who assisted me by reading early drafts, unwittingly providing crucial dialogue, challenging me to think more expansively, and helping me right the ship. I would like to believe I got there in the end, Tete. Many thanks. Much appreciated.

ABOUT THE AUTHOR

Andrew Chatora

Andrew Chatora is a Zimbabwean writer resident in England. He received an MA in Media, Culture and Communication from UCL. Andrew has written and published widely on topical issues with This is Africa publication. He is principally interested in the global politics of inequality which he interrogates through his writing. Diaspora Dreams is his debut novella. When he is not writing, he is working on his PhD thesis on Digital Piracy, with Birmingham City University's School of Media and English.

PRAISE FOR AUTHOR

Chatora gives us an honest account of the migrant's experiences in a world that seeks to silence him. Diaspora Dreams is simultaneously suffocating and isolating. Battle after battle, the reader is constantly thrown into the unforgiving world of a black man in a white man's world.
– Tariro Ndoro, Author, Agringada: Like a Gringa, Like a Foreigner.

***

Diaspora Dreams, a debut novella by Andrew Chatora, offers a re-fresh-ing and relevant voice on the immigrant experience. In a masterclass tour de force journey, the Zimbabwean born author takes us through the chal-lenges that arise from settling in different countries without any pre-existing social capital or other sources of support.
Diaspora Dreams lays bare the harsh economic realities and subtle racial barriers faced by recent migrants. The demands of family, the disintegration of families, and mental health issues are prominent features of these experiences, and Chatora paints these lived experi-ences brilliantly, showcasing his sublime skills as the consummate wordsmith.
– Patrick Masiyakurima, Author, Leicester University, United King-dom.

***

Diaspora Dreams, sheds a haunting light on the all-encompassing nature of racial prejudice and its minutiae permutations. A compul-

sive read which legitimately casts Chatora as an exciting addition to the emerging voices in African Literature.
There is little doubt this impressive debut heralds the arrival of an extremely talented and perceptive writer. Diaspora Dreams is dazzlingly real as it shines its light into the intricacies and emotional souls of the immi-grant community in Britain.
– Memory Chirere, Zimbabwean writer, essayist, and leading African literary critic and reviewer.

***

Diaspora Dreams explores the emotional nuance of the immigrant experience, as the narrative traverses through the different cityscapes of Britain.
–This is Africa (TIA).

***

Chatora writes brilliantly about expectations, loss, race, class, gender, family, and mental health illness...poignant subjects, but packs a hefty emotional punch.
– Gift Mheta, Writer, Durban University of Technology, South Africa.

***

Nuanced and evocative...A compelling exploration of the thorny conflicts that drive us apart and bind us – that's what Diaspora Dreams effec-tively achieves...
– Stan Onai Mushava, Author, poet, literary critic: In Memory of the Future.

ABOUT KHARIS PUBLISHING

KHARIS PUBLISHING is an independent, traditional publishing house with a core mission to publish impactful books, and channel proceeds into establishing mini-libraries or resource centers for orphanages in developing countries, so these kids will learn to read, dream, and grow. Every time you purchase a book from Kharis Publishing or partner as an author, you are helping give these kids an amazing opportunity to read, dream, and grow. Kharis Publishing is an imprint of Kharis Media LLC. Learn more at
https://www.kharispublishing.com.

NEW BOOK COMING SOON...

Smoke and Mirrors appears in a collection of short stories, **Harare Alcatraz and Other Short Stories,** a forthcoming anthology by the author. The anthology comprises a collection of eleven short stories set against a dual backdrop, one of childhood memories of what it entailed growing up in the early 80s in post-independence Zimbabwe's high-density suburbs and equally, the short stories also capture the author's vision of the black experience in exile in the United Kingdom, where he relocated after a few years teaching in Zimbabwe. Through diverse vantage points, lives of immigrants and first-generation Britons are highlighted in England as they tussle with mundane challenges and strive to make sense of their lived culture.

Read ahead for a taste of the author's upcoming immersive narrative short stories.

I

Smoke and Mirrors

I met Iffy at Wendover Heights Care Home, where we both worked, looking after vulnerable adults. She was Nigerian, and as a fellow African sister, we bonded instantly. However, when she asked me to marry her, a month into knowing her, it came as a complete shocker to me, especially as we were not going out, not even in an entanglement parlance, popularized by the anecdotal Will Smith, Jada Pinkett way. Besides, I had my wife Rudo at home with our two children.

I decided to hear Iffy out on why she had come up with this weird proposal. "What's this all about Iffy? Is this some kind of joke?"' I entreated.

"A joke? Do I look like I'm joking to you Onai?" shot back Iffy, "I know I've known you for over a month now, and in that month, you've proved yourself as a decent fella, whom we could do business with."

"Do business with what do you mean?" I was becoming more perplexed by the minute.

"I know about your wife and family, I'm not an idiot. It's not a real marriage I'm talking of here Onai," continued Iffy in a casual manner, as if she were talking about a mundane subject.

"You have dual Zimbabwean-British citizenship, don't you?" I nodded my head in affirmation.

"Right, so that's perfect for us; we would pay you whatever

amount you want to falsely get married to someone from any of the African countries we deal with. It will be a sham marriage. The idea is to get them into the country, allow them to settle into their own life, they get a job, acclimatise to their mundane lives here, after which you file for divorce. Or sometimes, it may be someone already in the country, and they don't have legal status. Dead easy Onai, all parties win, she gets her papers, you get your money, it's a win-win for everyone. Easy peasy," Iffy said, gleefully rubbing her palms together as if they were perpetually itchy.

I was horrified at how Iffy trivialized such a criminal act, as if it were merely something minor like shoplifting. "But that's human trafficking, isn't it? That attracts a lengthy custodial jail sentence. Besides, I run the risk of being stripped of my citizenship with the prospect of being deported to Zimbabwe," I interposed in annoyance at her blasé attitude.

"Well, suit yourself, Onai. I thought you had balls; I was obviously mistaken. When the bailiffs come knocking on your door for that £12000 plus debt you owe, don't say I didn't try to help you. But you're obviously a pussy; you can't be helped." And with that, Iffy walked away, leaving me stunned.

I was left conflicted though; her last statement on my debts certainly rang true. I had been dodging bailiffs over unpaid credit card loans, consolidation loans which had made me to sink further in the quagmire of debt. My wife Rudo wasn't happy because she wasn't privy to these debts. I had taken these debts to fund my secret mistress, Rumbi, back home in Zimbabwe, with whom I had a love child, Ernest, now four.

At the time Rumbi fell pregnant, I told her we couldn't get married, as she already knew I had another wife in England so that would be bigamy, I had remonstrated with her.

Rumbi had said, "That's your funeral to worry about, Onai. Perhaps you should have thought of that first, before you thrust your dick in me."

"I will not beg you to marry me or to be financially responsible for what's rightfully yours, but there are other ways to get your co-operation." And with that, she slammed the phone on me. I had a sudden feeling of de ja vu descending on me, following Rumbi's last cryptic remarks, which bordered on subtle threats. *But what could she do to me? She is in Zimbabwe; I live here in England, and the most I can do is see her here and there when I visit Zimbabwe. I will have the best of both worlds. Each time I'm in Zimbabwe, she'll be my comfort girl, and when in England I have the default position of my wife, mai Pamhidzai?* I rationalised to myself, and it seemed to make perfect sense to me. *Surely, what could go wrong?*

However, I may as well have been delusional, for barely a week after that cryptic phone call with Rumbi, I had the shock of my life when her very own father, Brigadier Pswarayi, phoned me from Harare. I was largely taken aback; I didn't think Rumbi would have had the guts to let her dad know she was pregnant out of wedlock, and with a married man, as well. I always knew, from what she said, that her father was a big shot in the army and the party, a very big man and not one to be trifled with. So, I sort of knew what was coming as I struggled to regain my voice over the shock of knowing the person on the other end of the line was my mistress' father.

"I will cut straight to the chase, Humba," barked the raspy, commandeering voice on the other end of the line, addressing me in my totem, which further disconcerted me. Something told me I was on slippery ground now, and it wouldn't be long before I would have the proverbial fall.

"You have some unfinished business with my daughter Rumbi, and I believe you are going to honor your filial obligations, both as a father to your unborn child, and your soon-to-be-second wife, Rumbi," he went on, much to my consternation that he knew about my other legitimate marriage.

"Ye…Yes sir," I stuttered, struggling to put words together, overcome by dread and fear.

"Now, here is the thing, Humba, I expect you to contact me at three months maximum, so we fix a date on when you can send emissaries to my family, so we formalize this thing with my daughter as your other, additional, subsisting marriage. It's fine by me; I am happy with polygamy; I have two wives myself. What I won't have is someone fooling around with my daughter and then thinking they can throw her to the wolves, just like that. No, it won't work; it doesn't work like that, Humba," he said, pausing to let that sink in. "I won't look for you again. Have I made myself clear, Humba?" He was almost bellowing down the line now.

"I've heard you, SaPswarayi."

"It's Brigadier Pswarayi," he corrected me, as if hammering a subliminal message to me.

"Brigadier Pswarayi. That's how you should always address me, Humba. I won't have to mention what would happen to your family and siblings in Mutare, if you don't play ball, Humba! Welcome to the family." And with that, the line went dead. He'd hung up on me.

I was totally gob smacked and flummoxed with these blatant threats from Rumbi's father. Something told me he wasn't bluffing, and I knew how these army bigwigs got away literally with murder in my home country. They were a law unto themselves, the military Junta, as we called them, and you were better off staying in your lane, rather than crossing their path. Mindful of these risks and the potential collateral damage on my family in Zimbabwe, I followed what I deemed the wisest course of action. Before the three months ultimatum was up, I sent a delegation of trusted *Sahwiras* from my family and thus paid damages and dowry in what could be termed my second marriage. All this was done under the veil of darkness and secrecy, as in England I was still legally married to my other wife, Rudo, and I didn't want her knowing of my bigamy, for obvious reasons. So even the selection of my delegation had been thorough pre-vetting, ensuring these were men who could be trusted to keep a big secret like this to themselves.

And so, the commencement of a double, duplicitous life began, in which I had two wives concurrently, one in England, the other one in Zimbabwe, though to allay my troubled conscience I always referred to Rumbi as my concubine or *small house,* as the colloquial parlance goes in Zimbabwe. In order to fund my secret life and support my other family in Zimbabwe, it meant I ended up relying on more secret loans and credit cards bailout. My live-in wife Rudo kept a sharp eye on the family's finances. Being a money monger herself, she was hawkish about money and it would have roused her suspicions, had she seen large sums of money leaving our joint family bank account.

The last couple of weeks in my personal life had been nigh stressful and difficult; my creditors and bailiffs were upping the pressure on me to pay up the outstanding arrears I owed on my debts. I had missed a couple of payments, owing to other domestic pressures again. And yet, here I was, Iffy had just presented me an opportunity to land myself £10000 or more, only if I played ball, but the stakes were high. I was well aware of that.

II

"I'm a survivor, I've always been a survivor," I consoled myself as I threw caution to the wind and phoned Iffy a few days later to meet up with me for a private follow-up meeting on her earlier proposal. Had I known my descent into hell was just about to commence, I should have stayed tight in my house. *But frailty, thy name is money*, I inwardly mused to myself as I took a seat at the back of Wing Restaurant at a quiet table for my rendezvous with Iffy.

I saw her coming through the sideway entrance. Iffy was quite imposing, an exceedingly tall, average lady, with a big bottom resplendent in her red dress, which made me to think of Chris DeBurgh's *Lady in Red* hit song. She flashed her radiant smile as she drew up the chair sitting opposite me. "You did well to have a re-think, Onai, thank you for accepting my offer," she said as she sat down.

This lady is smart, I couldn't help reflecting, as I chose my words carefully. "Well, let's just say, I didn't give you a chance, Iffy. Let me hear you out first, before we get ahead of ourselves by talking of non-existent offers and deals," I said, matter-of-factly.

"All yours, Iffy. What do you have to offer me?"

"You are on a no-need-to-know basis, Onai, so I'll spare you needless details. My colleagues I work with, let's just call them the Syndicate for now, we help out people without legitimate papers or visas in the UK, undocumented immigrants, if you're gung-ho on political correctness, which is where you come in. For a sham marriage organised by us and our allies in selected

UK marriage registry centres, we can reward you £10000 for your efforts." She paused, then asked, "Are you with me?"

"I'm listening. Go ahead, Iffy."

"I know your next question, 'What about my wife here in England?' We take care of that; we bribe our contacts in the home office, so they turn a blind eye to your marriage here, but we have a double insurance policy which is fool proof and ensures you're insulated from detection, in the event things go haywire," Iffy said. Then she added, "Because you were married in Zimbabwe, chances are your marriage is not registered here, so even if they were to check, nothing untoward would come up on the system. We carefully select people like you, Onai, because of this double lock insurance. So, if you're good to go, we can set the ball rolling. I've got a girl from Kenya. She's claimed asylum before, and it's been rejected, but our lawyers see marriage as a way out of her morass. Interested?"

"Let's not deal with ifs and buts here, Iffy," I said. "First, we agree on my payment figure and terms of payment, then we have a deal. Twelve thousand pounds is my asking price, half paid now and the remaining £6000 after completion of the wedding. Do we have a deal?" I remarked, looking her intently in the eyes. I was surprised I didn't even feel ashamed at my gradual descent into hell.

"We have a deal, Onai," Iffy replied confidently. She stretched her hand to shake mine as if to re-affirm her commitment to our deal.

"One other thing, Iffy, I will give you a secret bank account to transfer the money. I don't want to leave a money paper trail which will end up incriminating me. Once you've transferred the £6k, then you can proceed to fix the wedding date. But...but..."

"But what?" Iffy asked, "I thought we're agreeing all along, what's the but for?"

"This Kenyan girl, is she actually attached? Can we eeer...can we do it, if you know what I mean, as married couples, you know?" I remarked, a sly curl on my lecherous lips.

"Damn you, Onai, you pervert," Iffy chuckled. "I'll leave that to both of you, as you are adults. So, see how you both get on."

We shook hands again to seal our deal and Iffy promised to be in touch in the near future.

III

True to her word, Iffy kept to her side of the bargain. Within a few days I got a cash advancement of £6000 deposited in my Halifax bank account. Somehow, I felt a sense of unease and trepidation at getting the money. I knew there would be no turning back now. The die was cast, getting that money meant I had crossed the proverbial Rubicon. *Man up, pull yourself together man!* I said to myself in a bid to reassure my faltering conscience. I guess we all know it, when you cross the proverbial red line and start one's descent to the criminal underworld, and yet you continue to clutch at straws that all will be fine, it's really no big deal, whatever you are doing. But then, there is always that other voice, which we tend to push aside, as I did in my case.

The day of the wedding was set at Birmingham Registry Office, and Iffy and her syndicate had arranged beforehand all the preliminary paperwork to the letter. They were master connoisseurs, I had to grudgingly give them this muted adulation.

"We have an inside hand who will handle your 'marriage' with Assu, so remember to relax and act like a couple, okay. The day before the wedding, Wednesday, you will get to meet your future bride, Assu, at a pre-arranged secret venue in Birmingham, so we coach you into a dress rehearsal of the wedding ceremony for next day. Whatever happens between the two of you thereafter doesn't concern us, Onai. You and Assu are adults who can take care of themselves," Iffy said, winking with a conspiratorial, *you know what I mean smile.*

Assu was a looker from when I first set eyes on her, tall, stunning, super-slim with sharp pointed breasts whose nipples were threatening to rip through her flowery blouse and charcoal black skin, I felt something towards this stranger who was going to be my second secret wife, only this time, the repercussions were dire if I got found out. *I was getting to be a champ at these things, being an uncanny bigamist,* I inwardly reflected. "Hello, Onai," she said, extending her slim, slender fingers to my hand, as I stood transfixed, gazing at her, like I was a teenage schoolboy smitten by his first infatuation.

"Hello, Assu, pleased to meet you too." I pulled myself out of my reverie, but she must have known I was a goner already. I could feel a stiffening in my trousers and a disturbing palpitation of my heart. *What's happening to me?* I felt cross with myself for acting like a whopping teenager on a first ever date. We went in the foyer of the hotel in a quiet corner where we sat chatting amidst drinks. She was cool and sassy, with a knack for great conversation. By the end of the night, I knew I had crossed yet another proverbial line, and I felt helpless; I thought I wasn't doing myself any favours at all, getting attracted to a stranger who would most likely ensnare my life in further troubles.

We parted ways that evening. She retired to a different room, myself to my own quarters at the same hotel, where the syndicate would pick us up at 10am in the morning for a quick dress rehearsal before our registry wedding at 11:45am.

To my relief, the wedding reception proceeded ahead smoothly, without incident or drama. Assu and I were formally declared married, and the bit I had feared would turn embarrassing was when I had to kiss the bride. I closed my eyes as I kissed Assu's tender red lipstick lips. I must admit, I enjoyed it as my tongue rammed down her throat probing for inner orifices.

Within days, I was paid my remaining £6000 and I managed to halve off some of my debts. That was the end of this unsavoury business. Next would be filing for divorce and then I'll be rid of this sordid matter, or so I thought.

IV

Things went quiet for some time. I got back into my normal routine of life and in no time, two-and-a-half years had elapsed. I approached the syndicate puppeteer Iffy about starting divorce proceedings against Assu. Somehow, I had managed to surprise myself, as nothing had happened between myself and Assu, although we had kept in touch every now and then by phone, and once, I could say I detected some interest from her side. But I was a good boy. I didn't want to be presumptuous, lest I embarrassed myself. So, I let Assu's seeming interest in me pass by, pretending to play dumb.

"I wanted to raise you first, Onai. You beat me to it. It's in relation to Assu's spouse visa, there are some unforeseen changes you need to be aware of."

"What unforeseen changes Iffy?" I asked her curtly in an accusatory tone. My heart skipped, thinking maybe something untoward had happened in the interim.

"Nothing big, change of plan. Instead of you getting divorced from Assu, you will need to help her renew her visa first, after which you can go ahead with the divorce."

"But, but...that's not part of the original plan is it, Iffy? Why are you moving goal posts now?" I remonstrated with her.

"Calm down, Onai, that's why I said change of plan. There are some changes in the UK immigration laws which make it imprudent to divorce now, because it would prejudice Assu of her visa and potentially to remain in the country. So, to counteract that, you help her renew her visa after which, boom, the divorce goes ahead." Iffy spoke as if it was like opening and closing the door. Part of me resented Iffy for her manipulative streak, but I was far too gone in now, to try to feign moral outrage, let alone elevate myself on a pedestal. Inwardly, I knew I was now knee deep into this immersive shit, and merely thinking of this made me sweat inside.

I went quiet for a few minutes, after Iffy's expose. Something told me this was somehow a bad idea. Call it a premonition or a sense of foreboding, but that feeling was engulfing me.

I said, "Aaah, I want out of this whole thing Iffy. I've got a bad feeling about this. I've taken too many chances with my life, now I want a clean slate. My wife is expecting our third child and I don't want to mess up things now. I refuse to do it, Iffy, I want out." I was almost shrieking at her.

"Listen to you, Onai. Gosh, what's come over you? Pull yourself together," Iffy admonished. "Don't tempt me now."

"Tempt you to what?" I remarked, glaring at her. "What are you on about, Iffy? You call me, all mysterious and pontificating about change of plan. Why don't you just put your cards on the table?" I bellowed at her.

"Dare I remind you, there's no honor among thieves, and you're swimming in deep shit already, Onai. You're pretty much as compromised as I, so, there's no backing out now. You go ahead with this visa renewal thing, after which we can cut you loose. And don't you even think of pulling a fast one on us. You will receive the visa renewal pack already pre-filled with your personal detail information, Assu and yourself. All we will require of you is your signature, and you return the application pack back to us. Is that clear, *Mister whiter than white*?" Iffy sneered sarcastically at me.

I didn't like the tone in Iffy's voice, but I felt powerless to say anything. I was on shifting ground and I knew it. She'd got me by the balls; I was hanging right on my head, and she knew it, thus she enjoyed wielding her power over me, like the sword of

Damocles.

"What about the money?" I asked, somewhat timidly.

"Aaah, now we are talking. We are back in business, ain't we," she carried on with her biting sarcasm. "Now that it's only a renewal we need, we will determine what we give you, and there's no room for haggling. You get £5000 and that's it, end of story. I have to warn you again, not to try anything silly, Onai. You have more to lose, than I and my shadowy syndicate. You should be receiving the application pack in days, and the turnaround time from you is 24 hours." And with those words, she was off, leaving me perspiring heavily in the August heatwave.

V

I had a brooding sense of resentment and foreboding the next couple of days, even as I signed the requisite paperwork from the syndicate and promptly couriered it back to them. My wife Rudo noticed my aloof nature and enquired if all was well with me, but I managed to brush her aside. "All is fine, sweetie, it's just work-related pressure, otherwise, I'm fine," I lied in my bid to reassure her. She gave me a long, boring stare in my eyes, which further unsettled me, but then, there was no way I could come clean with my wife. The die had long been cast.

And then not long after that, one evening, it popped, in a very spectacular fashion for that matter.

"Honey, there are these men from UK Border Force and Immigration who've asked to speak with you," said my wife Rudo, as she ushered four burly looking police officers into the house.

"I'm afraid the game is up, Sir," remarked one of the officers, clicking his handcuffs on my wrists to the bewilderment of my wife Rudo and my two teenage daughters, Pamhidzai and Makanaka. I tried to blag it out and spoke with some false bravado. "It's some mistake love, I'll certainly explain it away and be back home in no time. In the meantime, can you phone Jenkins, our family lawyer, please?" I muttered as I was frog marched away in handcuffs.

Printed in Great Britain
by Amazon